ROS

Rose Tremain's novels and short stories have been published in thirty countries and have won many awards, including the Orange Prize (*The Road Home*), the Dylan Thomas Prize (*The Colonel's Daughter and Other Stories*), the Whitbread Novel of the Year (*Music and Silence*), the James Tait Black Memorial Prize and the Prix Femina in France (*Sacred Country*), and the South Bank Sky Arts Award (*The Gustav Sonata*). Her novel *Lily* was a Richard and Judy Book Club selection. Rose Tremain was made a CBE in 2007 and a Dame in 2020. She lives in Norfolk and London with the biographer Richard Holmes.

ALSO BY ROSE TREMAIN

NOVELS

Sadler's Birthday
Letter to Sister Benedicta
The Cupboard
The Swimming Pool Season
Restoration
Sacred Country
The Way I Found Her
Music and Silence
The Colour
The Road Home
Trespass
Merivel
The Gustav Sonata
Islands of Mercy
Lily

SHORT-STORY COLLECTIONS

The Colonel's Daughter
The Garden of the Villa Mollini
Evangelista's Fan
The Darkness of Wallis Simpson
The American Lover

NON-FICTION

Rosie: Scenes from a Vanished Life

FOR CHILDREN

Journey to the Volcano
Iron Robin

ROSE TREMAIN

Absolutely and Forever

VINTAGE

7 9 10 8 6

Vintage is part of the Penguin Random House group of companies
whose addresses can be found at global.penguinrandomhouse.com

Penguin
Random House
UK

First published in Vintage in 2024
First published in hardback by Chatto & Windus in 2023

penguin.co.uk/vintage

Printed and bound in Great Britain by Clays Ltd, Elcograf S.p.A.

The authorised representative in the EEA is Penguin Random House Ireland,
Morrison Chambers, 32 Nassau Street, Dublin D02 YH68

A CIP catalogue record for this book is available from the British Library

ISBN 9781529922509

Penguin Random House is committed to a sustainable future
for our business, our readers and our planet. This book is made
from Forest Stewardship Council® certified paper.

For Ginny and Elsa, dearest friends

. . . adoring love, the love of abdication,
is devastating. It takes up all thoughts,
all instants, it is obsessive, tyrannical.

~ Simone de Beauvoir, *The Second Sex*

I

When I was fifteen, I told my mother that I was in love with a boy called Simon Hurst and she said to me, 'Nobody falls in love at your age, Marianne. What they get are "crushes" on people. You've just manufactured a little crush on Simon.'

My mother's name was Lavender. Daddy called her Lal and I called her Mummy. I didn't like a lot of the things Mummy said. For instance, I didn't like her use of the word 'manufactured' in this context. If you manufacture something, a clear-thinking part of your mind has to envisage how it would look and sound and feel once you'd made it, but I had never envisaged the things I felt when I met Simon. I'd never thought for a moment that almost everything that had preoccupied me until then would be relegated to some fog-bound corner of my brain and that all the rest of it would fill up with my obsession with this one person. I'd never imagined that love could make me so totally stupid.

This was the 1950s. I was at a girls' boarding school called Crowbourne House in Hertfordshire in what we used to call England, but which now seems to be referred to by most people as the You Kay. In term time, at Crow-bourne House, we never saw any boys from one week to the next. But in the holidays, at home with Mummy and Daddy in Berkshire, I sometimes got invited to parties where we danced with boys to Tommy Steele records and drank cider cup. These parties were referred to as 'hops' by our parents. And this was how I met Simon Hurst – at a hop. He was eighteen, in his last year at Marlborough, and about to take his entrance exam for Oxford. The skin of his face was quite shockingly smooth and beautiful. He liked to let his dark hair flop over his forehead. When I danced with him, I felt as if I was being wafted to eternity.

After I met Simon Hurst, my sewing machine became my best friend for a while. I spent hours and hours and hours hunched over it, caressingly turning the handle and feeding into its obedient little bouncing needle pieces of shining grey taffeta. Together, the machine and I were making a beautiful dress. It came from a pattern by *Vogue*. It had a tight, sleeveless bodice, a bell-shaped skirt and a pert bow at its slender waist. When I wasn't making the dress, I was dreaming about how I would look when I put it on. The narcissism of a person in love knows no bounds. I began to see myself as I wanted Simon to see me, which is to say entirely and absolutely beautiful. When I looked in the mirror – even in the stained old looking glasses placed here and there in our school dormitories – I strained to recognise the lineaments of Cleopatra or Helen of Troy.

The first time I wore the dress was at a Christmas

4

party given by my friend Rowena Fletcher-Blake. When I arrived at Rowena's house, she said, 'Is that the thing you were making at school, Marianne?' She looked at me pityingly and this pitying look and the word 'thing' made my heart lurch. I wanted to reply that my dress was 'perfection' and that the pink and white fruit sundae of a gown which Rowena was wearing belonged on a fairground stall on Brighton Pier, but my throat constricted and I couldn't say anything. I pressed on through the throng of girls to where the boys stood awkwardly in a line, sipping cider cup. I told myself that in about two seconds I was going to see Simon and that under his adoring eye all my beauty and the splendour of the dress would return. But when I looked up and down the line, Simon wasn't there, and I immediately felt afraid, as though I'd been given news of a Russian nuclear strike on Berkshire. I didn't know what to do or where to go.

A boy called Henderson came out from the line and asked me to dance, so I did that, but I wouldn't let him hold me. He jigged around in an embarrassing way and I just waved my arms about, like I was trying to fly out of there, to wherever Simon was. After a while, Rowena's mother, Angela Fletcher-Blake, announced that a 'cold collation' had been served and everybody went into a different room and began to gnaw on chicken legs and scoop coleslaw into their pouty gobs, but I didn't feel hungry at all. I hung back beside an elderly woman chain-smoking in an armchair, enveloping the scene with grey-blue mist. I said to her, 'Do you totally love cigarettes?' and she smiled and said, 'Yes, I totally do. Do you?' I replied that

I hadn't yet learned to love them and that the only thing on earth I cared about was a boy called Simon Hurst.

'Simon Hurst,' she said. 'I know that name. I believe he once behaved badly with my granddaughter Rowena.'

'Behaved badly how?' I said.

'My dear girl,' she replied, 'I can't go into those kinds of details, but in my view, parties like this one only bring about the worst in boys.'

Now, the thought of Simon with Rowena – a thing I had never imagined – possessed me like an illness. I felt as if I might be sick, so I walked away from the grandmother and down a long hallway to the front door. This was a huge, haughty kind of house, with a gravel turning circle laid out around an old, complicated fountain, and I went out into the dark and walked towards that, wondering if I was actually going to puke into the fountain bowl. Then I saw the lights of a car come down the drive and I stood still, letting the bright white beams swish across me, as though I were taking part in a film. I expected the car to pull over and park, but it just slowed a little and came right on and stopped a few yards from me. The driver's door opened and Simon got out. He walked straight up to me and said, 'God, Marianne . . . angel . . . I'm so sorry. Did you think I wasn't going to turn up? Were you out here looking for me? Oh my darling girl, you're freezing . . .'

In an instant, my sickness went away. I clung to Simon and he held me against his chest and stroked my hair. 'I'm only late,' he said, 'because I drove myself and got lost. Look what we have here, in all its glory!'

He broke away from our embrace and took my hand

and led me to the car. By the floodlights placed here and there under big garden trees, I could see that he was showing me a Morris Minor, painted baby blue. 'It's mine!' said Simon. 'I told you I'd passed my driving test and now Mummy got me this. She bought it new, bless her. I wouldn't have opted for pale blue, but never mind. When I go up to Oxford, I'll be able to drive over and see you all the time! What d'you think?'

Still holding on to my arm, he caressed the Morris with his other hand. I knew he wanted me to caress it too, so I began stroking its lumpy little bonnet and I thought how sweetly ridiculous we probably looked, fondling a pastel-coloured car in the December darkness. And this felt like a secret thing between us, a thing that would take us to a different plane of our lives, so I said to Simon, 'Why don't we go for a little drive?'

Simon looked startled. 'What,' he said, 'd'you mean right now?'

'Yes.'

'And not go into the party?'

'Yeah. It's not a brilliant party. There's a grandmother who sits observing everybody and blowing smoke everywhere. And she told me you were involved with Rowena.'

Simon looked away from me, across to the house and its big lighted rooms. Then he said: 'I kissed Rowena. Once. It was before I met you.'

'That's all right, then,' I said. 'So, shall we get into the car? I like the smell of car leather.'

'You do believe me, don't you?' said Simon. 'It was absolutely just the one time.'

'Yes, I believe you,' I said. 'Does the car have a radio? We could have a little party of our own . . .'

'No. There isn't a radio. And won't you be cold? Do you want to go and get your coat?'

'No. I'll get it later, when we come back. I'll say I was feeling ill and you looked after me.'

I could see Simon hesitating, looking between me standing there in the semi-darkness in my home-made grey taffeta dress and the lighted windows of Rowena's house. Then he lifted my face towards his and kissed my eyelids and said, 'Are you sure this is what you want?'

We didn't drive very far. I knew we wouldn't. We came to a place where woods crowded in over the road, a place we both recognised, and Simon turned the car down a track leading away into the forest and stopped. In the car lights, I saw some animal creep away from us into the darkness and I thought, This is right, this is a moment nothing and no one must see. It will belong to me and Simon forever.

We climbed into the back of the Morris. From being still and trembling, we began to tear at each other and say each other's names in broken voices and I didn't know if I was crying or just howling out some feeling in me that was stronger than any I'd had, an elemental feeling, like a starving babe yearning and crying for human milk.

Then I found myself in a trance of pain. The skirt of my dress had been pushed up around my shoulders. I thought I could hear some of the stiches tear but I told myself that Rowena was right, the dress was just a 'thing', something a child had made, and what was happening to me now was a rite of passage into grown-up life. And then the pain diminished and there was just this beautiful movement of the two selves, Simon's and mine. I'd loved Simon for quite a long time, but that was when it really came pounding at me, my crazy, unalterable need for him, after we'd made love in the back of a Morris Minor, with the forest sighing above us and now and then the faint thrum of a car going by on the road. And I remember thinking, I don't want us to go back to the road. I don't want to think about Rowena or her grandmother, or dumb boys called Henderson sitting in a line, drinking cider cup, or about my mother trying to tell me what I felt. I want to lie very still and feel Simon's weight on me. I want to dream of a wedding. I want Simon to be dreaming of that, too.

After a long while, Simon said, 'I wish.'

'Wish what?' I asked.

'That you were older. That we could go up to Oxford together. Be proper lovers.'

'Wasn't that being "proper lovers"?' I asked.

'No,' said Simon. 'Because I had to hurt you.'

I remember that night so vividly, not just for the power of the first sex act of my life, but for the dilemma we faced after it was over.

We saw, after the lovemaking had ceased, that we were in a mess. There was blood underneath us on the leather seat and on the skirt of my dress. Simon found a brand-new duster in the glove pocket of the car and tried

9

to wipe the blood away, but the blood had congealed. We looked at each other helplessly. In my messed-up state, I couldn't go back to the party, but my coat was at Rowena's house and I had to get this somehow before my father came to collect me at eleven o'clock.

It felt cold in the Morris suddenly, and very late, as if hours and hours had passed without my noticing them. We sat side by side, holding hands and thinking. One thing I already worshipped about Simon was his ability to *think*. He said this talent only came about in his third year at Marlborough when he was taught by an English teacher who was a poet in his spare time and tried to convey to his pupils how much had been hidden from them in their sheltered lives. He'd told them that if they didn't start thinking for themselves and seeing the world as it truly was, in all its wonder and terror, they would grow up to be dull, unhappy men. Years later, when I thought about this person, I imagined him being like the Robin Williams character in the film *Dead Poets Society*, ripping out conventional thought from textbooks and venerating the work of Walt Whitman. If that picture had been around in those days and on that night when we sat shivering in the pale blue Morris Minor, I might have cried out, 'O Captain! My Captain, what are we going to do?' And yet part of me was calm. I thought, Simon will think of something . . .

I had no watch, nor did Simon, but by the faint blue light of the tiny clock on the dashboard of the Morris we saw that it was five past ten. The party would be winding down, with Rowena probably crumpling her fruit sundae dress against the body of some Henderson or other, at least one of the girls throwing up the cider cup in the charmingly appointed downstairs lavatory, and the grandmother lighting her seventeenth cigarette of the evening. And I thought, I am never going to go to another party in my entire life. I am just going to hide in some beautiful forest with Simon, like a vixen in a lair, and no harm will come to us.

After a few more minutes had ticked by on the blue clock, Simon said, 'Right. This is what we're going to do. I'm going to drive you home before your father sets out. We'll tell your parents that you're ill with a very heavy period – to explain the blood on your skirt – and that all we could think of was getting you home. All right?'

'What about my coat?'

'When we go into your house, I'll put my jacket round you, to hide the creases in your dress. I'll offer to collect your coat tomorrow and bring it over. If your parents see that you're ill, they won't worry about the coat. They'll just want to get you into bed and bring you Horlicks and aspirin.'

'OK,' I said. 'And anyway, I am ill. Love is a kind of illness, isn't it?'

Simon wasn't very good at reversing. We went in a zigzag back to the road. I imagined all the birds asleep in the wood, waking up and staring with their nervous little eyes at the wavering beams of light.

As he drove, I ran my fingers through Simon's hair and then through mine, trying to make us look neat and

11

innocent. We didn't talk. I felt so choked with love that my vocal cords seemed paralysed. I wanted to ask Simon if he was experiencing the same thing – a kind of petrification of everything, as though what we'd just done had brought time to a standstill. But I also liked the silence that had fallen on us and the way the grass verges along the road kept blossoming up into the headlights of the Morris, showing us an ordinary thing made momentarily beautiful in the darkness.

I had the powerful thought that we might never arrive anywhere, but just keep travelling on and on, side by side, mute and spellbound, inhabitants of an altered world. But far too soon, we reached my parents' house. I looked at its familiar aspect, a four-square kind of red-brick Georgian thing, with pretentious little white columns holding up a front porch and a birch tree on the front lawn which moved and sighed all the time, even on still days, and I thought, Well, we've arrived here, but my days as a girl in this house are numbered, because soon enough I'm going to marry Simon and travel the world with him and eat dates in Arabia and snorkel among exotic fish along the Great Barrier Reef.

The car drew up in front of the columns and we got out. Simon took off his jacket and hung it across my shoulders and I pulled it around me, loving the scent and warmth of it. He kissed my forehead and then we went into the house and found my parents playing Scrabble on a baize-covered card table in front of the fire. When we came in, they stared at us as if we were revenants from some distant snow-shrouded country and my mother jumped up and said, 'Goodness, you startled us. What happened, Marianne? Daddy was going to pick you up.'

I looked over at Simon, who was executing a little bow, as though he'd suddenly found himself in the company of the Queen or Winston Churchill, and then he straightened up and said, 'Really sorry to barge in on your Scrabble game. But I had to get Marianne home. She's not feeling well.'

My father was standing now and fixing Simon with that piercing look he'd perfected as a colonel in the Irish Guards. 'Get her home how?' he barked.

'In my . . . well . . . in my . . . uh . . . *car*, sir,' said Simon.

'*Car*?' said Daddy.

'It's a Morris Minor,' I said. 'Simon's mum gave—'

'What kind of "not well"?' interrupted my mother.

'Just the . . . you know . . .' I said. 'But I felt really sick and faint. Luckily, Simon was there . . .'

'Sick and faint,' said my mother, 'oh dear, my poor child, and that dress you made all ruined! Say goodnight to Daddy and let's get you into bed, pronto.'

My mother came bustling round to me and started to take Simon's jacket off my shoulders, but I clung on to it. 'I'm cold, Mummy,' I said. 'I forgot to collect my coat. What I'd really love is a hot bath. Could you run me a bath and then I'll come up?'

'Morris Minor?' said my father suddenly. 'Any bloody good, is it?'

'Oh, the Morris,' said Simon. 'Well, it's my first car, so I'm not really in a position to know.'

'Underpowered?'

13

'Um . . . I don't know. It probably is, sir.'

'I've heard they're underpowered. Feeble torque. But steady on the road, is it?'

'Yes. Pretty steady, sir. Got Marianne home in one piece.'

'Don't *quiz* the boy, Gerald,' said my mother. 'He's done very well. Give him a ginger beer while I go and run Marianne's bath.'

She hurried away. Daddy said, 'Ginger beer? Not sure about that. How old are you, Simon?'

'Eighteen, sir.'

'Bloody right. Whisky for you, I would have thought. No longer an infant, what?'

The next time we met was at a birthday party for Simon's little sister, Jasmine.

Jasmine had been an afterthought in the sex lives of the Hurst parents, so she was only nine. She was a crazy kind of little girl, never still, throwing her body about in the attitudes of a ballet dancer or imagining she was a bouncing ball or sometimes a karate champion. Simon adored her. I could see very clearly the look of sweet affection on his face whenever he was with her. He told me how he'd sit for hours in her rickety tree house, pretending to drink tea with her dolls and teaching her to play gin rummy. And this was something else that I began to love about Simon: his patience and kindness towards Jasmine.

This was a daytime birthday party. How we were going to pass the afternoon was by taking part in what the Hurst parents, Marigold and Christopher, called a scavenger hunt. We were divided up into teams and sent out into the lanes of Berkshire with a list of things we had to find and bring back. One of the things on the list was a worm. Others were: a stinging nettle, a round stone and a piece of chalk. Another was a piece of 'Ancient Iron'. You couldn't take any tools or utensils with you; you had to use your hands or find a stick or a stone with which to dig things up. All you had was a paper bag from Bartlett's of Newbury in which to put your finds. The team who got back first with the full list got prizes. These prizes consisted of identical wooden pencil boxes, wrapped in crepe paper and tied with garden string. When Simon saw Ancient Iron on the list, he said to his mother, 'Most of these kids are nine years old, Mummy. And you're expecting them to come back with Saxon arrowheads?'

'Not necessarily Saxon, darling,' said Mrs Hurst, whom I was now encouraged to address as Marigold. 'Just rusty bits and pieces that look old. The farmers round here leave lots of industrial debris lying about. It shouldn't be too hard.'

'It will be hard,' said Simon. 'I'm crossing "Ancient Iron" off.'

'Then you won't win. Don't you and Marianne want to win?'

'No. I want Jasmine's team to win.'

'Then why not join your teams together? When you're clear of the others, you and Marianne go and find Jasmine and the Bellingham girl, whatever her name is.'

'Her name's Belinda.'

'That's it. Belinda Bellingham. Rogue of a father. You three go together and help Jasmine. I know it's cheating a bit, but why not? It's her birthday. Don't you think, Marianne?'

I said I thought it was up to Simon and the moment I uttered these words, I felt as though I'd said something fatal. It was like I'd suddenly understood that I'd lost control of my life and put everything into Simon's hands. I felt myself get very hot, with a raging blush spreading over my face and neck. I turned away. We were standing by the front door, where a row of wellingtons was lined up, and I bent down, pretending to examine these, to find the right size for me, but they all looked way too large and sort of heavy-seeming, so I didn't know what I was doing there staring at them.

I heard Marigold say, 'I don't think you'll need wellies, Marianne. Weather's been very dry.'

'Oh,' I said, without moving from my bent position, 'yes. Right. So, no, we don't need boots, but excellent, we're partnering with Jasmine and Belinda?'

'If they want us,' said Simon. 'They might not want us.'

'They will want you,' said Marigold. 'And head up towards Squirrels' Tump. Lots of Saxon arrowheads lying about there.'

Marigold laughed and winked at me and I had to unbend myself and join in with her laughter. I put my hands to my face to cover up its embarrassing burning. 'And,' said Simon, 'it's too early for stinging nettles, Mummy. Didn't you do Nature Studies in between

16

straightening your stocking seams and learning to dance the Charleston?'

It was a sunlit winter's day, the beech woods grey against an infinity of blue sky. Jasmine went tumbling ahead of us, turning cartwheels, her plaits flying about in the breeze, and Belinda Bellingham charged forward with her head down like a rugby player, or like a little bullock, struggling to catch her up.

Simon took my hand – the one not holding the still empty Bartlett's bag – and tugged me behind a tree and we kissed in a fierce little frenzy. Then we went walking on, keeping Jasmine and Belinda in our sights, and I thought, This is how it will be when we're married. We'll have two children, girls probably, and they will go running ahead of us and we'll feel proud of them and build a tree house for them and buy them school uniforms from the Army & Navy Stores, but our great love will remain here, in our hands clasped together, and there will never be any love that feels stronger than this.

We headed for Squirrels' Tump, the steep, grassy hill where Marigold had said we might find bits of iron which the farmers had left lying around. We told Jasmine and Belinda to 'comb the ground' for iron and shiny round stones and to start digging for worms, but they couldn't find any of these things and quite quickly they seemed to forget all about the scavenger hunt and just wanted to roll down the tump, over and over, shrieking and laughing, then climbing back up and rolling down once more,

17

covering their clothes in bits of grass and dry mud and flakes of old cowpats.

Simon watched them with a tender eye. We sat down at the very top of the hill. It must have been cold there, yet I don't remember feeling that it was. When I turned my face towards Simon, he said, 'I want to kiss you, but I'm not going to because then I'll want more,' and I felt a kind of swoon come over me at these words. I reached out and touched Simon's hair, the lock of it that fell almost over his eyes, and I said, 'Do you think we'll always love each other?'

He didn't look at me but gazed out very intently at the fields and hedgerows below us, as if trying to commit them to memory. Then he turned his face to the sky and took a deep breath of the bright air. And later I remembered this moment and my unanswered question and how Simon seemed to be taking photographs of Berkshire in his mind and how I then said, 'I think I'll always love you, Simon. Absolutely and forever.' And how Simon turned to me and smiled.

The next time we met, just before the spring term began, was at a hop given by my friend Cordelia Pratt, where we smooched to Ella Fitzgerald records and when the song 'I Could Write a Book' came on, Simon said, 'That's it really. That's what I'd like to do with my life: become a writer.'

This statement made me feel inadequate. I didn't know how to respond because I couldn't imagine how writers underwent *becoming*. The writers we mainly studied at school were Shakespeare and Dickens and it had never once occurred to me that there had been a time in their lives when they had had to *become* what they eventually were. I couldn't even imagine them as young men with shiny heads of hair, wondering what thoughts to scribble down, but only as they appeared in portraits, with wrinkles around their eyes and peculiar beards, and in Shakespeare's case, a bald head like a speckled boiled egg.

I forced myself to picture dapper young Charlie Dickens trip-tripping along Piccadilly, twirling an ebony cane, and scruffy young Will Shakespeare getting hammered on sack in a riverside tavern and falling into the Avon. But I couldn't quite picture either of them actually writing anything; they were too keen on just being alive and having brilliant thoughts about themselves. On the other hand, I was able to imagine Simon crouched over a typewriter in some isolated room crammed with books and sheets of paper. He *was* working – or trying to – and I immediately put myself into the picture, in the role of his obedient servant, bringing him cups of Nescafé and chocolate digestive biscuits and emptying his ashtray into a waste-paper bin. What I couldn't figure out was what he was actually trying to write about or how his words even got onto a page that had started out completely empty and blank.

We danced on. Cordelia, who was a good friend and never criticised me like Rowena Fletcher-Blake, and who understood how things with Simon had become so serious and irrevocable, came over to us and whispered,

'Mummy and Daddy have gone to the pub for a couple of hours. My room is the second on the right after the stairs.' So we slipped away and went into Cordelia's room, which was still like a child's room, with two rag dolls on the bed and wallpaper of little intertwining roses and violets. We sat the dolls on a chair and I saw them watching us with their moons of faces and painted-on eyes. We undressed completely and got into the bed and this time we made love more like proper grown-ups, not tearing at each other as we had done in the car, but staying calm and letting all the feelings and movements happen slowly. And then when it was over, Simon had a kind of crying fit and I didn't know why.

We could hear the music going on downstairs and we were feeling hungry, so we got up and dressed very carefully and set Cordelia's bed to rights, with the dolls lying side by side and gazing up at the ceiling, like Simon had gazed up at the sky on the day of Jasmine's scavenger hunt. It was pitch-dark in the hall, where the dancing was, so we just glided into the throng, unnoticed, and clung to each other and after a while Simon said, 'Did we miss supper? Do you think Mrs Pratt made a cold collation?'

The term began and I resumed my boarding-school timetable, which hardly varied from one day to another. The first thing that happened in the day was that a thermometer, tasting of disgusting Dettol, was shoved into your mouth by one of the three matrons. You could hear the matrons approaching your bed by the sound of their crackling starched uniforms. They circled your dormitory, passed on to the next one and then came back to take the thermometers out again, read them in the semi-darkness and returned them to the Dettol cup. There were a hundred girls in the school and about thirty thermometers, so each thermometer went in and out of three mouths every day, which was a repulsive thought. Lots of girls, including me, yanked the thermometers out of their mouths as soon as the matrons had crackled their way out of the room, and this was the moment – with my disinfected thermometer in my hand – when my brain reminded itself that all it cared to do was to think about Simon.

This happened every single morning. I'd wonder what, exactly and precisely, he was doing at Marlborough. Was he getting dressed and combing his hair into its gorgeous floppy style? Was he walking along some draughty school corridor on the way to breakfast? Was he thinking about me as he walked? Or had he got up early to revise for his Oxford entrance exam? Was he already reading some desolate and complicated Greek play which I knew I would never understand?

When the thermometers had gone, we queued up, clutching threadbare towels, in the freezing bathrooms to wash in cold water and put on yesterday's clothes. This included yesterday's knickers and often you'd see girls sniffing these knickers before they put them on, hoping they weren't too embarrassing. And now I remembered what my knickers smelled like after making love with Simon and how I'd found this unfamiliar scent of sex intoxicating, like a perfume that had come out of the earth, and then I felt pity for all the other girls who had not yet known this and never would for a long time to come.

After breakfast, which was sometimes a kind of quite bearable hash we called 'bacon pudding' and sometimes just runny tinned tomatoes on squares of fried bread, gulped down with weak coffee or dishwash-grade tea in plastic beakers, we went to our lessons. I'd told myself that I would work harder than usual at these, especially at English and history, so that I wouldn't seem dumb to Simon when half-term came round and would be able to hold a conversation with him about the uncool behaviour of my namesake Marianne in *Sense and Sensibility* or about the role of the heralds in the Battle of Agincourt, if he chose to have one with me.

In English that term, we were studying *Romeo and Juliet* and because I identified with Juliet, who was even younger than me when Romeo became her lover, I began to try really hard to understand the play, looking up words I didn't know and saying lines aloud to myself. The character I liked most in the first part of the drama was the Nurse, who understands what Juliet and Romeo are doing and what they feel, and I kept thinking how I wished that I had somebody like the Nurse in my life, somebody much kinder than Mummy, so that I could snuggle up to her and sit in the shelter of her arm. I imagined her listening attentively while I confessed to her that my head was so burdened by my obsession with Simon that I was afraid of becoming a total imbecile. And she would stroke my hair and reassure me that this was a perfectly normal state for young people to be in, that we were all inevitably headed for a stay in the Love Asylum, but that in time the spell would be overcome and normal life would resume.

The form of madness which overtook me very soon after term began was a longing for letters from Simon. He'd told me when we were at Cordelia Pratt's party that he'd write to me 'every day' and I think I'd believed him. But it soon occurred to me that, with the Oxford exam looming, he might not have time to do this. He might be too tangled in the French subjunctive tense or in the biological composition of the liver fluke. Nevertheless, when a week of term had passed and no letter from Simon had come, I began to feel that some tragedy was approaching me and I got this sensation of suffocation in my chest.

Simon had very tiny writing. The letters were perfectly formed, but titchy little miniatures of themselves, like angels trying to stand on the head of a pin. My longing to see my name written on an envelope by these angels grew so acute that my body began to feast on that, as if yearning were a substitute for food. I couldn't swallow the bacon pudding, only take sips of the weak coffee and wait for that to return some strength to me.

After nine days, it came. I couldn't believe the thing I wanted so much was actually there in my hands:

Miss Marianne Clifford
Form V
Crowbourne House School for Girls
Buntingford
Herts

I opened it with tender care, as if the envelope was a sentient thing. To my disappointment, the letter was a bit short. It began *Darling Marianne*, but then it just went on to tell me news about a rugby match the school fifteen had won and about a new boy in the Sixth Form called Amar Nath Chatterjee who had come over from India and who was *cleverer than anybody else alive*. I thought Amar Nath Chatterjee was the most brilliant name I'd ever heard and I paused in my reading of the letter to wonder whether if you had a fantastic name to live up to, this increased your intelligence quota without you really noticing it. But then I hurried on, looking for reassurance that Simon was thinking about me as much as I was thinking about him. At the very end, the letter made a kind of coded reference to the things we'd done in the Morris Minor and then in Cordelia's bedroom, but it didn't say what I was hoping for, which was a declaration of undying love. So then more than ever, I wished I had a wise old Nurse to comfort me and tell me what I should say in my reply.

I went to the library and took out a volume of Greek tragedies by Aeschylus. I didn't even know how to pronounce the word 'Aeschylus', but I wanted to impress Simon by quoting something, so that he'd think me worthy of being introduced to Amar Nath Chatterjee. I found some lines I liked in a play called *Prometheus Bound* about some poor guy chained to a rock for stealing the fire of somebody or other. The lines were: *'The sun shall scatter the hoar frost again at dawn, but always the grievous burden of your torture will be there to wear you down, for he that shall cause it to cease has yet to be born.'* I was going to write that my adoration of Simon was exactly like this, like the hoar frost melted by the sun at dawn but then returning and returning and never giving me any rest. But then I saw that to describe my feelings as 'torture' was a bit extreme and also how the whole thing would make me look pathetic and abject.

Instead, I wrote a sane and quiet little letter, describing the scenery Form V were painting for our production of *The Mysteries of Udolpho* by Ann Radcliffe. I put:

> *We're making huge panels out of sugar paper on wood supports so that the wings and the back wall appear to be a castle. We're confecting spiders out of pipe cleaners, painted black, and spiderwebs out of string. What we're hoping for is that the whole school gasps when the curtain goes up. I am playing the part of a man, Signor Montoni, an Italian brigand.*
>
> *All my love,*
> *Marianne xxx*

Letters to and from Simon went back and forth – letters which I kept tied by a piece of scarlet ribbon – and then we came to the moment when Simon had to go to Oxford to sit the entrance papers. I sent him a little glass pig, which I'd used as a mascot for my end-of-school-year exams. Accompanying the pig, I put in a card that said *I am thinking of you at Oxford and sending my lucky pig to watch over you*, and I liked to imagine him holding the pig tenderly and then putting it on the desk or table or whatever he had to sit at to write the exam papers, feeling his nerves calmed by it. But I never found out if this was what he'd done or whether he'd just left the pig behind in his school locker with his geometry set and his supply of illicit Woodbines.

What happened next was so unexpected, so grave, it brought along with it a feeling of catastrophe. It was as though we'd been flying along in a BOAC aeroplane and the plane suddenly began to nosedive towards the earth in a long and fatal fall.

Simon failed his Oxford entrance.

I learned about this in a letter from him dated 7th March 1960. I took it into the empty Prep Hall to read it. Simon's already titchy writing had got even smaller, as if he could hardly bear to dirty the page with it. He told me that he'd been all right when he arrived in Oxford and walked along the river, thinking about me and imagining me lying in a punt while he poled us along in the sunshine. Then the moment of going into New College arrived and he felt very cold, suddenly, and when he sat down in the draughty hall and lined up his pens on the desk, he saw a mouse running back and forth, back and forth along the wainscot, and after he'd seen the mouse, he couldn't get his mind away from this verminous little creature and onto the exam questions. When he tried to write his answers, he knew straight away that they were inadequate and that he would fail.

He said that everything – his whole life – now seemed arid and pointless. He'd been so sure that he would go up to Oxford in the autumn that all he could see in front of him was a precipice. He said: *The worst thing is an over-whelming feeling of shame. And Mummy and Dad can't conceal from me that they feel it too – that disgrace is afflicting the family – and I know that they don't know what to do with me. I think they just want me to die.*

I read the letter four or five times. There was a smudge on the word 'die' which might have been a tear, and then what I thought about for a moment was Simon crying in Cordelia Pratt's bed and how this had been strange but beautiful. But I knew I had to get on with some kind of reply. I got out my rough book and tried three or four versions of a letter, but I was repelled by how clichéd were the workings of my mind.

After some long miserable minutes, I found myself clutching at the idea that Simon would kill himself and then I would have to kill myself too, and this might be a relief because then we wouldn't have interfering parents meddling with our future, but would ascend to heaven together in the pale blue Morris Minor, with my head lying on Simon's lap. I could see the advantages, like never having to understand the plays of Aeschylus, never trying to figure out how Aeschylus came to become what he became, nor how I or Simon would become whatever we were still hoping to become when all the Oxford sorrow had faded. *Becoming* was just too hard.

So I wrote more or less this: I said I wasn't sure how one went about committing suicide, but that I was quite ready to die, provided we could do it together, side by side. I told him that for as long as we remained alive, I

27

would love him, but if we had to die, then this was all right and I would probably wear the grey taffeta dress that I'd slaved over for so long in the school sewing classes because a torn thing, with a virgin's blood still staining it, felt sort of right for the occasion.

Then I read through what I'd written and scrunched it up. I saw that I came across as a foolish, melodramatic person and I couldn't believe that Simon Hurst could love someone like that. It felt wiser – if my thoughts were so inappropriate – to stay silent, but I knew I couldn't do this either. I had to say something.

I left the Prep Hall and went down to the office of the school secretary, Miss Veitch, and asked permission to make a telephone call. You were only allowed to make calls if they were 'matters of family urgency'. I told Veitch that this was 'beyond urgent', that it was the call that would prevent someone from dying.

'Who is this "someone"?' Veitch asked. 'Is it a family member?'

'Yes,' I lied. I wanted to say that this was my future husband, but instead I said Simon was my cousin and told her about the mouse running back and forth along the wainscot and the failed exam. She looked shocked, as if I'd said something rude, but she gave me two shillings out of my pocket money allowance for the call and I went to the payphone with its old-fashioned Button A and Button B and dialled Simon's house.

Marigold answered. At the sound of her voice, I remembered that thing she'd said about Saxon arrowheads and I thought how on that day of the scavenger hunt we'd all been in a state of innocence, not knowing that something as small as a mouse could destroy the life you'd planned. Marigold sounded very distant and cold. She said she'd have to see whether Simon would come to the phone to talk to me because, since the Oxford shock, he wasn't really talking to anyone, not even the dog. She went away and I hung on, wondering how long the two shillings would last. Then Simon came on the line and said breezily, 'Marianne. How did *The Mysteries of Udolpho* go? Were you a convincing brigand?'

I put the second shilling in the money slot and said, 'Simon, I've been trying to write to you, but my words seem to come out all wrong.'

'Who played the heroine?' asked Simon. 'Emily, isn't she called?'

'Oh,' I said, 'Rowena played her. But let's not talk about that. I'm so sorry about Oxford. I totally understand that you feel like dying. If it's any comfort, I'm totally on for dying as well. If you wanted—'

'Let's not talk about it, Marianne,' said Simon. 'I don't want us to talk about it any more.'

'No, but I only wanted to say—'

'Everything's ruined and that's it. My whole future's gone down the sink. There's no virtue in discussing it over and over again. I'm going to Paris at Easter.'

'Paris? Why Paris?'

'I have to find another route into my life. And Mummy wants me gone. She can't stand looking at me.'

'Simon, I'm sure that isn't—'

'I've been enrolled at the Sorbonne in some course on

Civilisation: French literature, history and philosophy. But I probably won't see it through. I'll just hang out in jazz clubs or try to meet Sartre and Simone de Beauvoir and get drunk on existential nihilism.'

'What's existential nihilism?'

'It's the Philosophy of Nothingness in the godless world. *Le néant*. Very popular in France. And it's the place I've reached in my life.'

After that there was a silence. Because I didn't know what to say about existential nihilism, I just stared out at the rain and I wondered if it was raining in Berkshire and if Simon was staring at it too. A long time seemed to pass. I could hear Veitch in her office bashing away on the huge old typewriter and I thought, A woman like her has never known what it's like in the Love Asylum, and maybe she's fortunate. I felt myself beginning to cry. I tried to tell Simon that I loved him, but all that came out was a ridiculous gulping noise, and then the second shilling ran out.

We saw each other one last time.

It was Easter Day. The beauty of Simon, with the rainbow light falling on him from the church window, was difficult to behold. He looked over to me and I thought I could see him thinking how disappointing I was in my entirety. But when we came out of the church, he broke away from Marigold and Jasmine and came and took my hand and led me away among the tilting tombstones. Jasmine turned and came bouncing towards us, wearing a straw hat circled with white ribbons which fluttered in the springtime air, but Simon told her to go away.

We stood beside a yew tree and he put his arms around me and said, 'I'm never going to forget you. Never.'

I said, 'Will you write to me from Paris? Even just a postcard.'

'I don't know,' he said. 'I don't know what's going to happen to me.'

'Well,' I said, 'if you can't write to me, I could get on a ferry at the end of term and come to Paris, and we could go on the river in a punt—'

'Don't!' said Simon. 'Because everything's changed. Better to just move forward. And one good thing has happened. I've started writing. Just short stories. I don't suppose they're much cop – too miserably autobiographical. But if I'm lucky enough to meet Jean-Paul, I might dare to show him some of my stuff.'

'Who's Jean-Paul?' I said.

But Simon didn't answer. He put a little kiss on the tip of my nose, the kind of kiss you would plop onto the face of a baby.

If you were at a boarding school like mine, the only bit of time you looked forward to was the summer term, because then the place itself – the gardens and the park – took on a kind of temporary beauty. Daisies came up everywhere, even on the grass tennis courts, where they weren't meant to be, and they scented the air with an innocent perfume, like talcum powder, and there were roses scrambling over all the ancient walls and pink candles swaying on the chestnut trees.

The teachers (who were referred to as 'mistresses' in

those peculiar days, when England was still known as England and not the You Kay) liked being outside in fine weather, so we would often have lessons sitting in a circle on the grass, with our legs sticking straight out in front of us, and I sometimes thought that we resembled dolls. The mistresses brought out old wooden chairs from the Prep Hall so that they could be comfortable while they discussed the odes of John Keats or the workings of a trebuchet in medieval siege warfare and not be distracted by the sight of their legs or the pain in their spines. But they were distracted by other things: by blossom falling from the cherry trees, by swallows turning above the school turrets, by wood pigeons calling from the spinney, and sometimes they stopped the lesson and told us to be still and quiet and look and listen and be thankful for the beauty of England.

I didn't like these moments. I refused to be thankful for the beauty of England when Simon wasn't in it. My thoughts would drift towards Paris, which I imagined as a place where everybody said philosophical things all the time and never bothered to study medieval siege warfare. I would position Simon at a café table, with the sun slanting across his soft brown hair and a French cigarette in his hand and people talking and laughing all around him. And then I would feel quite ill with a longing to be there beside him, even if I wouldn't be able to understand a word that anyone was saying. I would know that when that particular day was over, Simon and I would make love in some attic room, with lace curtains at an open window moving gently in the summer breeze.

Sometimes, our period of thankfulness for the beauty of England would end without my noticing and the lesson would resume and I would still be in my Paris reverie and one of the mistresses would say, 'Marianne, sit up straight, please, and pay attention.' But it was difficult to come back to the lesson and I knew that, as the term went on, my concentration on work was very weak and that I was falling behind the class in almost every subject, except French. Here, in the French lessons given by an actual French person we addressed as Mam'zelle Charrier, I wanted to climb inside her head and extract in its entirety the library of sounds it contained so that when I went to Paris, I would astonish Simon and all his new friends with my fluency in a language unknown to me until now. One day, I asked Mam'zelle Charrier if she could give me extra coaching in the hour after lunch when we had to sit around, knitting garments for a charity caring for orphaned babies, while we digested our meal of mince and cabbage, but she shook her head and said, '*Non*, Marianne, *désolée*, but I am not paid to do that.'

'I could pay you,' I said.

'What with?' said Mam'zelle. 'Smarties?'

Rowena Fletcher-Blake and Cordelia Pratt, who had once been on holiday in Brittany, had already informed me that French people were rude and mocking, especially to English people, whom they referred to as 'Anglo-Saxons', as if we were all still ignorant barbarians, wearing chain mail, but I somehow couldn't think of them like this and I knew that Mam'zelle was just making a little joke,

33

so I smiled and said, 'What I mean is, I could ask my parents to pay for the coaching, if you had the time.'

Mam'zelle reached out and patted my shoulder kindly. 'Well,' she said, 'you ask them and then we'll see.'

I wrote to Daddy. There was no point in writing to Mummy because Daddy controlled what he always called 'the purse strings' and I think only gave Mummy money when she asked for it – for her hair appointments and her cookery classes and her 'girls' lunches' at the Kardomah in Reading and other things like that, in which Daddy took no interest. I explained to Daddy that Simon was expecting me to visit him in Paris in the summer holidays and that I didn't want to *let myself down* by being hopeless at French, so could he please pay for some coaching from Mam'zelle Charrier. I felt that this sounded reasonable. I thought that Daddy liked Simon, even if he'd been a bit critical of his car, so I expected him to agree, but I was absolutely wrong. What I got from Daddy was a curt, almost cruel note telling me to stop my *Simon Hurst nonsense*. He told me that under no circumstances would he and Mummy pay for French coaching or allow me to travel to Paris. He said I was far too young to have a boyfriend and that anyway, *Simon has let his family down very badly by flunking Oxford after that hugely expensive education he was given* and that he, Daddy, would be extremely disappointed in me if I didn't put him out of my mind and concentrate on my own life, *as befits a girl of your age and upbringing*.

So then it seemed to me as though Paris had suddenly been relocated to Africa or somewhere, to a continent thousands and thousands of miles away, which I would never reach. I stopped trying so hard in Mam'zelle's lessons. I stopped annoying Rowena and Cordelia at Lights Out by saying '*Dormez-vous bien*.' There didn't seem to be any point to anything I was supposed to be doing. I just gave my heart to my knitting – doing one stitch and then another and then a thousand others, and at the end of it having a little garment known as a matinée jacket, badly sewn together but good enough to keep an orphaned baby warm.

When the summer holidays came, we drove to Cornwall in Daddy's Rover. We stayed with friends of Mummy and Daddy's called the Forster-Pellisiers, who had one son called Hugo and a Dalmatian dog called Sparky. The Forster-Pellisiers had rented a white villa on the clifftops near Padstow. The white villa was so big, they had to try to fill it up with people, but it felt to me at first that they didn't actually and truly love us, so it occurred to me that perhaps they were a bit short of other friends, or that their other friends found their name ridiculous and just couldn't bring themselves to say, 'We're going to stay with the Forster-Pellisiers.' Or perhaps I was wrong and the Forster-Pellisiers always enjoyed our company, but were just not the kind of people who showed that they enjoyed things. I thought I could see that they liked drinking pink gin at sunset with Mummy and Daddy on their huge terrace, and I overheard them telling the Cornish postman that 'Colonel Clifford had a very good war, you know, exceptional war.' So then I thought that it was probably because of Daddy's 'good war' that they put up with me and encouraged Hugo (a freckled, orange-haired boy of seventeen) to teach me to play table tennis.

The table-tennis table was situated in the garage. In between the bouncing and swiping of the little white ball, Hugo Forster-Pellisier and I began exploring all the stuff that had been stored in the garage for the summer by the owners of the house. One of these things, among boxes of china, leather suitcases, broken toys, Meccano kits, squash racquets, surfboards, fishing rods, torn silk cushions and a Roberts wireless, was a rail hung with women's clothes, and for reasons which I can't exactly name, we enjoyed looking through these and laughing at the garish colours of the dresses, and one day we took two fur coats off the rail and put them on and Hugo said, 'This is the game now – we've got to see who can win at ping-pong wearing a fur coat.'

My coat was sheepskin, with bits and tatters of grubby wool hanging off it, right down to the floor. I tried to imagine how many sheep had been sheared to make this coat. Hugo said I looked like a yeti and began to giggle. He put on his fur, which was astrakhan, and I told him he reminded me of a huge lump of anthracite and we laughed some more and gave each other nicknames, which were Yeti and Anthracite. In the enormous coats, our table-tennis skills became pathetic and all we could do was giggle, and I thought in the midst of this hurting laughter how for at least twenty minutes I hadn't thought about Simon and I felt really grateful to Hugo.

After a while, Hugo decided to plug in the Roberts

wireless and the Light Programme came on and began playing 'Bye Bye Love' by the Everly Brothers and we sat side by side on the ping-pong table, still wearing our furs and jiving with our arms. Remembering the song from Cordelia's hop and my lovemaking with Simon in her bed, I was beginning to get my sad Simon longing once again when Hugo said, 'I don't know why every single song is about love, do you? Why aren't there any songs about stamp collecting?' And this brought back our giggles and when the song ended, I leaned over and gave Hugo a kiss on his freckled cheek. I said, 'You're a good egg, Anthracite,' and he said, 'You're nice to be with, Yeti,' and so we kissed very lightly on the mouth and I kind of enjoyed this, and I found myself thinking, I'd better stay here with the Forster-Pellisiers for as long as possible and then I won't keep dreaming about being in Paris with Simon.

The weather was very hot. One morning, Hugo and I stole two surfboards out of the garage and climbed down the steep cliff path to the beach below and stripped off to our bathing costumes and walked towards the sea, not looking at each other's bodies, then began riding the waves. The feeling of being carried on my board by the roaring breakers made me excited and reckless and I kept going further and further out, so that the ride would hold me for a longer time.

Towards midday, it amused me to see, from far off, Mummy and Daddy and Mr and Mrs Forster-Pellisier (Jocelyn and Felicity) arriving at the beach, taking small, hesitant steps, like old people, and carrying an armoury of deckchairs and sun umbrellas and a mutilated old picnic basket with which to set up a bivouac on the sand, while the dog, Sparky, stood quivering at the sea's edge, barking at the waves. I called to Hugo and said, 'You know something? I'm never going to become like the parents. I'm going to live in Paris and meet Simone de Beauvoir.'

'Who's Simone de Beauvoir?' asked Hugo.

'Oh,' I said. 'Don't you know anything, Anthracite?'

'I know more than you, Yeti,' said Hugo. 'Your father told me you don't work hard enough at school.'

'He told you that?'

'Yes.'

'Well, I think that was mean of him. You're my friend, aren't you?'

'Yup. I'm your friend. And I liked it when we did the kiss. Did you?'

'Yes.'

'Do you want to do more stuff together?'

'No. I don't know . . . The thing is that I'm soon going to live in Paris.'

'Why does that make any difference?'

I felt confused then. Part of me wanted to tell Hugo that I was totally and absolutely in love with Simon and always would be, but I also didn't want to put Hugo down and make him look like a loser, because he didn't deserve that. So I just pretended I hadn't heard his question and said, 'I just can't believe Daddy said that thing about my not working at Crowbourne House. I thought parents were meant to be loyal to their children.'

38

'Well,' said Hugo, 'I think he thought he was being loyal. He thought it might help you to talk to me about it.'

'Help me how?'

'We could ... I don't know ... do some history together. Help you catch up.'

'That's kind of you, Anthracite,' I said, 'but I'd rather play ping-pong.'

'Up to you, Yeti,' he said. 'But I'm quite strong on George III and the loss of the Americas.'

Surfing makes you very tired. When Hugo and I were called back to the beach by Mrs Forster-Pellisier (sorry, Felicity, I meant to say), we could hardly walk. We flopped down on the sand like pale pink seals. Daddy said, 'Well done, children. Nobody drowned so far,' and Mummy said, 'Don't get sand in the picnic.'

I liked the feel of the warm sun on me and the sensation of my heart beating fast but quite strongly. It was as if the surfing had put some medicine into my blood and I thought, This would be a moment of pure happiness if only I could let myself stop remembering why happiness has become impossible for me. I closed my eyes and listened to all the sounds of the beach: the waves crashing in, the gulls making their *pew-pew* noise high above us, the faint laughter and little cries of other families, the dog, Sparky, chewing a rubber bone, Felicity Forster-Pellisier opening the creaking old picnic basket and Mr Forster-Pellisier (sorry, Jocelyn) popping open a bottle of white wine. And I thought, I'm going to try to let happiness in, just for a while.

*

While I was in Cornwall, I prayed that when I got home to Berkshire, I'd find a letter from Simon. On the long drive home in the Rover, I imagined the envelope, with its blue-and-red airmail border, waiting for me on the table in the hall. As we drove across Salisbury Plain, my vision of the letter somehow eclipsed my view of the standing monoliths of Stonehenge that had waited patiently for me to see them for four thousand years (or perhaps longer, for all I knew about them then). From this, I have to conclude that love makes people indifferent to even the noblest feats of primitive engineering, but that they feel no real remorse about this.

When we pulled up at the house, I wanted to run straight in and grab the letter, but Daddy had mislaid the front door key, so I waited by the shivering birch tree while he searched for it in the car and Mummy lit a cigarette and paced up and down to stop herself from feeling cross. I felt furious with Daddy. I found myself wondering how he'd managed to have 'a good war' if he couldn't even remember where he'd put the key to the house, and I almost said this aloud – 'I don't know how your war can have been good, Daddy, if you can't even . . .' etc . . . etc . . . – but I felt this was too mean and I knew also that I didn't know anything about what Daddy had actually done in the war, because he never talked about it, apart from being wounded in Germany in 1945, and I didn't want to risk being mean to a hero of the Irish Guards.

He eventually found the key in the glovebox of the Rover and we trooped in, carrying our suitcases and, in my case, a shrimping net which had been a gift from

Hugo Forster-Pellisier when we went to Treyarnon pool to look for baby crabs. I threw the net down on the stairs and ran to Daddy's study, where I knew the post would have been laid out for him on his desk. And there it was: the miraculous airmail envelope, with a French stamp on it, addressed in Simon's titchy writing: *Miss Marianne Clifford, Hastings House, Weston Applegate, Nr Newbury, Berks*. I snatched it up and held it against my cheek and all my longing to be in Paris came surging back, so that it was as if the Cornwall episode had never happened at all.

The letter was beautiful. It described the room in the rue de Grenelle where Simon was lodging and where, in his small bed, he thought about me 'an awful lot'. He told me he was sorry for being 'cold' when we said goodbye in the churchyard and how angry he felt with himself for messing up Oxford and finding himself so far away from me. Then it said the most unforgettable thing:

I have sometimes suggested to myself that the love I feel for you can't last because we're both so young and know so little about the world, but I've come to hope that it will last and that, at some point in the future, we will be together.

I read this sentence over and over until I'd memorised it. It was forty-eight words long. I knew that whatever else I was forced to think about over the next bit of time, these forty-eight words would always be there in the back of my mind, like a song that keeps playing and never ends.

*

41

The day before the autumn term began, Daddy gave me what he called a 'dressing-down'. He was in his colonel mode, standing very upright and looking down his long nose at his wayward daughter. He said, 'If you don't pull yourself together, Marianne, and decide to work at your lessons, I am going to have to take steps.'

While I waited for him to tell me what those 'steps' would be, he lit a du Maurier cigarette with his Dunhill lighter and puffed angrily on it. I stared at him. His face looked very red, as it always went when he was cross, and I imagined how, in the war, the men of his regiment may have been frightened of this redness of Colonel Clifford and tried to stand straighter or salute or something, or start polishing up the buckles of their uniforms. I didn't have a buckle to polish, so I just stood there, by the window of his study, waiting to be told about the 'steps' and feeling tempted to say to him, 'Schoolwork doesn't matter. I'm never going to do anything clever or useful. I'm just going to become Mrs Simon Hurst. That is my only plan.'

But I kept quiet. I thought about the night of Rowena's hop and the thing Daddy had apparently said about Simon's Morris having weak torque. I had no idea what torque was, but I wondered if 'weak torque' was a metaphor for something else, something really snarky that Daddy wanted to say to Simon. But then I remembered that he'd given Simon some whisky while I went up for my bath and how Simon had told me that he'd been 'pretty decent' to him and thanked him for bringing me home safely. So I began to say, 'Listen, Daddy—' but he cut me off and snapped, 'Don't interrupt, Marianne! I haven't finished. This tendency of yours to interrupt me when I'm talking seriously to you is extremely irritating. You aren't yet sixteen years old. You know nothing. I pay good money for your school, but your reports are always disappointing. So I'm telling you now, I'm giving you one more term, one more chance, and then I am going to have to take steps.'

'I don't know what you mean,' I said.

'Well,' said Daddy, 'I'll tell you what I mean. Your mother and I have decided we are going to have to take very serious steps if you don't knuckle down. I could not be more clear about this. I hope you understand me.'

'I'm trying, Daddy,' I said. 'But you haven't told me what the "steps" are.'

'Don't be impertinent! You will soon enough find out what they are and I'm telling you now, you won't like them. So I want you to promise me that this coming term you will work hard at every single subject and come home with a school report you can be proud of.'

I looked away from Daddy. Outside his study window was a bird table which Mummy always hung with coconuts and bits of bacon rind and I saw that a very beautiful bird had arrived there and was feasting on these things, but I didn't know the name of this bird, just like I didn't know what 'torque' was, or how to pronounce the word Aeschylus or actually remember whether this playwright was Greek or Roman, and so then the thought came to me that perhaps I would have to try harder to grasp more things about the world. The wonderful name Amar Nath Chatterjee came back into my mind – Simon's clever Indian friend – and I decided that although I didn't know Amar Nath Chatterjee, I would endeavour to become more like him by studying harder and learning the names of birds and car parts and old playwrights and religious feast days across the world and the works of Simone de Beauvoir.

'There's only one thing,' I said, turning back towards Daddy.

'What?'

'I really would like to do extra French coaching with Mam'zelle Charrier.'

'Absolutely not,' said Daddy. 'Now go away and think very hard about what I've said. Or else.'

When I told Rowena and Cordelia about the 'or else', they both gave a kind of snort. Rowena said, 'That's typical of parents. They never know what to do about it when we disappoint them.'

Cordelia said, 'They hate us underneath. Didn't you know that, Marianne?'

'Underneath what?' I asked.

'You know. Pretending to care about us and paying for dental work.'

'But why would they actually hate us?'

'Because they know that they're the past and we're the future.'

I realised that this was quite an astute thing to say, even though it hadn't crossed my mind until that moment, but when I thought about my future as Mrs

44

Simon Hurst (riding a camel in Egypt, floating along in a gondola in Venice, driving through the Grand Canyon in an open-topped Cadillac, watching elephants drink from a waterhole in Africa) and about Mummy's future (in the red-brick house in Berkshire with the shivery birch tree and the two white columns, playing Scrabble with Daddy and shopping at Bartlett's of Newbury), I could see that my life was going to be more interesting than hers and that she might already be envious or even jealous.

But I did decide to work harder. Not to avoid Daddy's 'or else', but because I wanted to get a bit more brainy. I was in the second year of O levels now, with girls who knew a lot about the English Civil War. I didn't want to admit to them that I hadn't really known there *had been* a civil war, but just vaguely thought that Charles II just took over from Charles I. One of them, called Mandy Fraser-Kidd, said to me, 'What do you think the word *restoration* means, then, Marianne?' And I had to be honest with her and say, 'It's a thing Daddy says when he needs a drink: "Need a bit of *restoration*, old thing."' And Mandy laughed a mocking laugh and said, 'You'd better wise up a bit or you'll never pass the exams.'

I'd sort of forgotten about O levels, but I soon enough had to remember them. At that time, you didn't have to take maths or Latin, so I just threw these things away from me, like too tight clothes that pinched my breasts. Before I met Simon I had chosen English and French, with a kind of back-up of history, geography and biology. Five subjects seemed quite sufficient for me to master. I kept remembering how hard Simon had apparently worked at ten or eleven different subjects and how in the end all this wasn't enough to equip him for the Oxford entrance exam and so, in retrospect, the hours he'd spent learning Latin verbs and doing chemical experiments and a hundred other things appeared to have been in vain. But I knew that he admired clever people and that it might be embarrassing for him to have a wife who knew nothing about the Bayeux Tapestry or the Peterloo Massacre. Also, I got just gently interested in history. I said to the history teacher, Miss Nelson, 'The reason I like this subject is because everything in it is safely in the past, so I don't have to get worked up and worried about it,' and she replied that she thought this was 'a very odd and ignorant attitude to have and really not true at all'.

I asked why it wasn't true and she said, 'History is a continuum. Think of Mrs Pankhurst. Where would we women be without those who fought for women's suffrage?'

'I don't know,' I said. 'Where would we be?'

'In the Dark Ages, Marianne. Without any power at all.'

I said that I didn't think we really had any power anyway. I told her that when Mummy exerted any power, like daring to win a Scrabble game, Daddy got into such a red rage that it was easier and more peaceful for her to keep on losing. But I could see that Miss Nelson thought this was pathetic. Her face contorted itself into a horrible sneer, so I changed the subject. I asked her if she was a descendant of Admiral Nelson.

'Ah,' she said, letting the sneer subside, 'the great

Horatio. I wish that were true. But we can't change our heredity, alas.'

'No,' I said, 'but we can change our future names. My future name is going to be Mrs Simon Hurst.'

Miss Nelson shook her head. She had on her face the kind of despairing look people have in public places when they lose control of their screaming toddlers.

'Go away, Marianne,' she said, 'and try to grow up and start thinking for yourself.'

The thing my 'self' mainly thought about, as the term wound on into the autumn, was getting letters from Simon. Sometimes he sent cards instead of letters, with pictures of Paris on them, and I passed these round to Rowena and Cordelia and to a new friend I'd made called Petronella Macintyre, known as 'Pet'. Pet was Scottish and quite snarky and rude and this made me laugh, so sometimes Pet and I would snark together and be rude about everybody else in our class, and this always cheered me up, particularly in weeks when I didn't get a letter or a postcard from Simon. When I told Pet that I'd lost my virginity to Simon in the back of a Morris Minor, she said, 'Och, *that*. Well, don't think you're special. I got rid of mine long ago, but it was in a Vauxhall and the stud was named Duncan.'

Pet was very good at riding and so was I. I'd been worried that Daddy's 'Or Else' might eventually translate into a cancellation of the riding lessons he paid what he called 'good money' for, so I'd prepared myself to say, 'Riding is the one and only thing I'm good at, Daddy, so please don't take it away from me,' but this didn't happen, so Pet and I and a couple of other younger girls were all put into a minivan on a Friday afternoon and bused to a riding stables near Hertford.

The horse I loved was a black filly called Mirabelle. I felt cross if anyone else was allowed to ride her because I convinced myself that Mirabelle and I had a kind of affinity and that she reciprocated my love. When the lesson was over, I'd put my face against Mirabelle's nose and whisper words of affection to her and I loved the way she always stood very still while I whispered them. Pet's horse was a stallion called Merlin, which was about seventeen hands tall, but Pet showed no fear. We were learning to go over small jumps and the thrill of this sometimes made me want to scream. At the back of the riding stables was a lovely grass meadow and at the end of the afternoon, Pet and I were allowed to gallop around this as fast as we could on Mirabelle and Merlin, a little Derby with a field of two, and I used to imagine I could hear the trees cheering. Merlin the stallion always won the race against Mirabelle because that's what male people and animals do: they always win. But I didn't mind.

I worked as hard as I could at French. Sometimes, when I didn't understand what Mam'zelle Charrier was saying, I felt like crying. Between one language and another there seems to be a kind of wall and you have to keep chipping away and bashing at this wall and bits of the wall fly off all the time and wound you when you make mistakes. It gets to feel so painful and exhausting, you want to lay your head in a gas oven and breathe sweetly till you breathe no more. I kept cursing Daddy for not paying for special coaching. Whenever I got a picture of Paris from Simon, I carefully inserted myself into it – a tiny little dancing figure, wearing black drainpipe trousers and a matelot top, swinging her ponytail along in the autumn breeze – but the idea that, if I were actually there, I wouldn't know how to talk to anybody or understand what they were saying was unbearable. One day, I said to Mam'zelle, 'Isn't there some kind of shortcut – a way of just getting the language into me without really trying?'

'*Non*,' she said. '*Cela n'existe pas. Comme vous le savez très bien, Marianne.* Just as there are very few "shortcuts" in a human life.'

I thought quite a lot about this. I wondered if Oxford had been a kind of shortcut to a brilliant life for Simon and now that he'd missed it, his future would somehow lack the thing he'd yearned for, even though he might not be able to say exactly what that thing had been.

More and more, as the term went on, I spent time with Pet and not with Rowena and Cordelia. They reminded me too much of Berkshire and boys called Henderson, whereas Pet was much braver and wilder than them. Even her hair was wild and looked as though it had been a bit scorched in some kind of fire among the Scottish heather. One day, Pet and I stole a cup of vegetable oil from the kitchen and bathed her scorched hair with this and she said, 'That feels like angels' balm.'

Later in the term it was to Pet that I confided the awful

49

thing that was now happening to me, day by day: Simon had stopped writing to me. Pet looked at me solemnly, the way people are supposed to look in a church service. 'When did you last get a letter?' she asked and I told her it was three weeks and four days ago. I'd written back, telling Simon about trying to smash down the wall that stood between me and the French language, but I'd never had any reply. Pet said, 'Let me look at the photograph of Simon again and I'll see if I can read his mind from that.'

Simon had taken a black-and-white photograph from a drawer in Marigold's desk to give me as a memento, 'to last until we see each other again at Christmas', and it showed Simon in all his gorgeousness, with his wide-apart eyes, his curvy mouth and his brilliant hair flopping over his wide forehead. Pet stared at the picture. I said, 'Behind the smooth skin of that forehead lies a fantastic mind,' and Pet said, 'Don't go overboard, Marianne.' I said that it was far too late to say that; I was completely 'overboard'. I explained that my whole being was bound to Simon's and always would be. Pet shook her head. Then she went back to looking at Simon and after about two solid minutes of looking at him, she said, 'You know, all this makes me afraid somehow.'

'Why?' I asked.

'I can't exactly say,' said Pet.

'Try to say.'

'I can't. I would if I could. But one thing I agree about: Simon Hurst is beautiful.'

She handed back the photograph, which I always kept under my mattress and sometimes looked at in the school night, when the moon made a coming-and-going kind of visitation to our dormitory. Now, when Pet said there was something which made her afraid, I got the feeling that a stone had lodged itself in my chest and was pressing on my heart. I wanted to cry but knew that crying wouldn't take away the pain of the stone or move it one single inch. Pet seemed to see exactly what I was feeling and she put her arm around me and pressed my head down onto her shoulder and I liked the smell of her navy blue cardigan and the heaviness of her arm holding me close, but the tickling of her scorched hair against my cheek made me want to pull away from her and scratch my face.

I arrived home at Hastings House on the nineteenth of December 1960.

That date is still carved into my brain.

The minute I went into the hall, which was decorated with the ancient Christmas tat Mummy strung up each year, I saw the airmail envelope on the table. I snatched up the letter and ran up the stairs to my room.

Dear Marianne . . .

I almost didn't need to read on. A letter that began like this could only be telling me something which would implant the stone in my heart forever.

Dear Marianne,

I'm so sorry not to have written sooner, but I thought it best to wait till you got home and could read this there and not at school.

I am getting married.

My fiancée is my landlady's daughter, Solange Louvel. She and I became very close almost as soon as I arrived in Paris. She is twenty-two. We are getting married in Paris after Christmas. Solange is expecting a child in June and being of a Roman Catholic family, of course she must be married to the child's father. I hope you will understand that this is my duty and not feel too angry that the future we thought that perhaps we had glimpsed together will not now happen.

I believe I will always think of you. I am remaining in Paris, which I feel is a kind of 'home' now, so I don't know when we will meet again. Please take care of yourself.

Simon

II

I'm not quite sure how I got through the next bit of time. Sometimes, a memory or a dream of 1961 and 1962 flickers into my mind and I glimpse the ends of things – always the ends: the burning of Simon's letters, the hockey match lost, the applause for a school play, the last riding lesson with Mirabelle, the A-level exam papers left almost blank on a little square table, a walk with Pet down the school drive and both of us singing 'Arrivederci, Roma . . .'

Then it's 1963 and I'm in London. I'm nineteen years old. Mummy enrolled me in a secretarial college and rented me a basement flat in Bayswater. She bought me a few things for the flat: a stainless-steel kettle, an iron and an ironing board, a Denby casserole dish, some wooden spoons and a green eiderdown. She said, 'Daddy and I are counting on you to make a new start now. We had to pay a lot to get you on this course, so you can't mess it up like you messed up your entire school career. You know that, don't you, Marianne?' Then she drove away. This is another ending that comes often into my mind: Mummy driving away in a new beige car. I went down the basement steps to my flat and curled up under the green eiderdown.

The secretarial college was in South Kensington and at lunchtime I would sometimes walk down Sloane Avenue to the King's Road, where what I had known as 'normal life' now looked completely different and abnormal and wild. I'd sit in the Picasso coffee bar trying to adjust my mind to this alteration.

It seemed to me that everybody in that place had undergone a metamorphosis which made them appear entirely beautiful in a deranged kind of way. Especially the women. Their hair was so mighty, I just couldn't imagine how it had got like that. Their faces were mainly very pale and thin, with eyes rimmed with kohl. They wore tiny little slanty boxes for skirts and their legs, underneath the boxes, looked as though they had grown like the pale roots of lilies, in order to curve down into soft white leather boots. In these shining boots, they tripped along, with their candy-pink lips open and smiling, admiring their own reflections in the windows of the new shops, from which surged the kind of music that nobody had ever heard before.

The guys sauntering up and down the King's Road were sometimes with the girls but more often on their own, like lone gazelles. These men, with the kind of long, soft manes which would have made Colonel Clifford gag and want to 'take steps', looked as though they'd never worked in an office and might not even know what an office was, but just preferred to be here, doing nothing much, only delicately pawing their way along in velvet trews and snakeskin boots, smoking and laughing and letting the autumn sun enhance their radiance.

Sometimes, groups of this new species of creature came into the Picasso, and as they passed me, I caught the scent of them, strong and bittersweet, and I kept wondering and wondering what their trick had been, to become the people that they were now, with such a love of themselves and of the present moment. I knew that I envied them. It looked to me as though they had never had their hearts broken, never yearned for things that were lost. More than this, they seemed to announce that the future was entirely theirs and that nobody else would find a proper place in it. When I caught sight of my own reflection, in some space behind them, I understood that I, and people like me, who made their own dresses from an out-of-date *Vogue Pattern Book*, who had only moderately nice hair and who knew so little about the world, would probably never escape from the shadows that they cast.

Once, I went into one of the clothes shops and stared at the rails of tiny skirts. I took one down and held it against me and then put it back. I tried on some huge, soft hats, draped with chiffon, and stared at the skin of my face, which, ever since Simon's marriage, had broken out into spots and now looked like some kind of lumpy grey soup insufficiently blended in Mummy's Kenwood mixer. Wearing one of the beautiful hats, I found myself moving gently to the loud music that was coming out of the shop wall and, for a moment or two, I quite liked the feeling of being able to keep time with it and lifting my arms above my head. But then I remembered dancing with Simon at Cordelia's hop, dancing to the Everly Brothers' 'Bye Bye Love' before we went up to Cordelia's bedroom and made love like grown-ups, and I suddenly needed to sit down because I was faint with sadness and I looked all around the shop, but there were no chairs, so I took off the hat and sat down on the floor and just cried quietly while other girls barged about all around me, laughing together, trailing an unfamiliar perfume and carrying armfuls of clothes on wooden hangers.

On certain days, particularly when I was in the typewriter room of the college and fifteen typewriters were clattering and pinging and the carriages were being shunted left to right, left to right, and the wall clock was clicking away time, measuring our typing speeds, I felt my mind disintegrating. I thought, I'm in a madhouse; life has brought me here, to an asylum of a kind. It wasn't the old and wondrous Love Asylum, it was now the Grief Asylum, where my heart was being shunted back and forth, back and forth, inside a chamber of despair.

I kept trying to type, but all I wanted was to get out of there – not to go anywhere in particular, but just to walk down the stairs and out into South Kensington and perhaps up Exhibition Road as far as the park and then somehow *not to be*. Lately, I'd often thought about dying and wondered how people went about it. The trouble was, I knew I was a coward. I could see this very clearly. I was actually terrified, not of dying, but of the *process* you had to go through to reach death. I began wishing that phone boxes weren't phone boxes at all but convenient little euthanasia booths, where you pressed Button A and a lovely lethal gas scented with privet flowers overcame you, and that was that.

The only thing I still liked doing was eating. I couldn't really afford the spaghetti Milanese at the Picasso, but sometimes I afforded it anyhow and told myself that running up debt was just part of the ways and means of getting through grown-up life. I thought that, in the end, Daddy would probably pay off my overdraft. He would say his stuff about how I repeatedly disappointed him, but then he would pay – because he could afford to and because he didn't want me to start stealing money and go to prison and he would have to tell his friends in Berkshire that he had a criminal for a daughter.

I began to drink red wine with the spaghetti Milanese and I found that this could send sudden little flares of hope into my brain and I would start to delude myself that I had a plan for my future. I'd picture myself in different foreign cities: Rome, Madrid, West Berlin; never Paris. There I was, tripping along in the sunshine, with big hair and the skin of my face healed and peach-perfect, while young people on Vespas sped past. I walked with the confidence of a girl who has formed a coherent idea of who she is and how her life will unfold. But this was really all my plan consisted of: a kind of hologram of me, heading towards some consoling destination of the mind, which, in actual fact, I was unable to name.

I was on my third glass of red wine on a Tuesday lunchtime at the Picasso when one of the gazelles sat down at my table. He was wearing dark glasses and a skimpy ribbed top, undone far enough to show off his dark chest hair. He had a camera strung round his neck. He said, 'I've seen you in here before. Why are you always alone?'

He put one hand on my elbow, which was resting on the scuffed surface of the old Picasso table, and I saw that this hand was very long and white and beautiful. I said, 'I suppose that's just how it's turned out.'

He said, 'I've noticed your skin. I could cure that for you.'

A waiter came by and the gazelle stopped him and ordered a bottle of Chianti Rosso and two glasses. Then he turned back to me and said, 'Do you believe me?'

'Believe you about what?'

'That I could cure your acne.'

'No. Nothing cures it. I've been told it will go away in time.'

'And you're happy to walk around like this?'

'No. I'm not happy about anything.'

'But drinking wine makes you feel better?'

'Drinking and eating. And I suppose that's all we are in the end, just bodies, consuming stuff to stay alive.'

'Oh, you haven't heard, then?'

'Heard what?'

'This is the Age of Love. Free love. Love cures everything.'

We drank the Chianti and chain-smoked Peter Stuyvesant cigarettes. Everything in the Picasso began to take on a roaring kind of beauty. I was meant to go to a shorthand class at two o'clock, but when I got up to leave, the gazelle, whose name was Julius Templeman, said, 'No, no, that's not the deal. Don't you want to try my cure for your skin? I mean, what have you got to lose?'

We walked out into the King's Road. A Beatles track was being played in a shop selling nothing but beads and silver ankle chains and feather boas: '*Love, love me do . . .*' Near this shop, just down Walpole Street, Julius had parked a little black 2CV with one of its rear wheels up on the kerb. In this attitude, the car reminded me of a dog, lifting its leg to piss. I thought how weird and disgusting a lot of my private thoughts were becoming, but I seemed to know that there was nothing I could do about this. Grief can make people revolting and that's just a naked fact. When my grandmother Violet died, Mummy suffered a terrible episode of acid reflux and her breath became foul in a very short space of time.

I got into the doggy car and Julius drove in a bumping and lurching kind of way up to North Kensington and down into one of those little mews places which always seem silent and composed, waiting for something to happen there. While Julius searched in his man-bag for a key, I began to feel dizzy and I knew that the thing which was going to happen in this mews was that I was going to fall over and find myself in utter darkness.

When I woke up, I was in a bed with black satin sheets and Julius was beside me, sleeping, with his beautiful white hand lying on my naked shoulder. I lay completely still, trying to recollect the things I'd done or not done in the previous bit of time, but my mind refused to remember anything after I'd got into the car. I looked around the bedroom, wondering where my clothes were. My head ached and my body was cold.

After this meeting with Julius Templeman, I tried harder to become like one of the skinny King's Road girls. Julius told me he was a well-known photographer, even though he was unknown to me. He said when my skin cleared up he'd take my picture. So for him, or for the idea of the photograph he might take of me – I'm not quite sure which – I stopped eating proper meals and lived on green apples and Ryvita and cigarettes. I bought four miniskirts and kohl for my eyes and thick make-up to cover my acne. Part of me wanted Julius to fall in love with me and another part was completely indifferent to him. Whenever I let him make love to me, I felt tortured by shame. Then one night, as I lay very silently underneath him after the sex thing was over, he said to me, 'I never told you this before, Marianne, but you are actually a lousy fuck.'

It was winter by the time he said this. I told him I was sure he was absolutely right. I got out of the black satin sheets and dressed as quickly as I could. I said a very polite goodbye. Near the bed was a standard lamp with a huge purple lampshade made of satin and I had the odd thought that even if I lived to be old, I would remember the look of this lampshade, its precise colour and the clod of cold light that it shone onto the floor of Julius Templeman's bedroom.

I went into the living room, which had a high ceiling going up into the roof, and looked at Julius's photographs around the white walls. Mainly, they were pictures of one particular girl. She had enormous eyes underneath a heavy fringe and a luxuriant smile which showed off her perfect teeth, and I thought perhaps she was the girl whom Julius had loved, but who had left him to get married to someone else and now he was reduced to trying to love people like me, whom he picked up in the Picasso, because he was lonely.

It wasn't too far to walk from the mews to my flat in Bayswater, but for some reason, my vision felt impaired. The street lamps seemed to illuminate only tiny little triangles of the world and the parked cars looked like mounds of hay. I turned around every now and then, hoping to see a taxi light, even though I didn't have enough money for a cab, because struggling along in this quaint, freezing darkness brought on an intense feeling of suffering which was hard to endure.

No taxi light came by. I realised after a while that my eyesight wasn't defective; I was just walking through a thick fog of the kind Simon had once mentioned as belonging in the works of Charles Dickens. Until now, as a child of Berkshire, where the air was clean, I'd sort of imagined that London fogs only existed in the great author's imagination, but here I was, feeling my way towards Bayswater, with this dense and suffocating mist clamped over the world, haunted by the idea that I might be lost forever. I had no idea what the time was. I remembered suddenly that I had to sit a shorthand exam the following day and the thought of this made me hurry along a bit faster so that some hours of rest might be mine before I had to go through this ordeal, if only I could find my street and my basement steps and my door. I didn't think at all about Julius Templeman or about being 'a lousy fuck'. I just yearned to be warm again and close my eyes.

We were coming to the end of the autumn term. What faced us before Christmas, as well as the shorthand tests, were typing SAs or 'Speed Assessments'. My SA score was meant to be twenty-five words a minute, but I couldn't seem to get my allotted Remington to go that fast without making jumble after jumble of mistakes. Miss Brent, the typing instructor, would perambulate approvingly along the rows of girls, all trying to be as deft as concert pianists, but when she got to my chair, she would look over my shoulder at the gobbledegook emerging from the Remington's keys and her hand would shoot out and grab the paper from the platen and wave it in front of my eyes and scream, 'What *is this*? I simply have no idea what you think this is, Marianne. I am in despair!'

The despair of Miss Brent was echoed by the despair of Miss Macauley, who taught us Gregg's shorthand. When I'd asked her why we were learning Gregg's when every other college taught Pitman's, she'd replied, 'Gregg's is the aristocrat of encrypted systems,' but I found that I hated it very violently. What I hated most was not the array of symbols we had to learn but the things those symbols symbolised. The thought of a life spent taking down phrases like *yours of the 2nd inst.* or *unfortunately at the present time* or *please find enclosed said accounts for your perusal* could bring on a choking feeling in my heart. Sometimes this pain was so severe, I had to lay my head down on my desk and close my eyes, and bits of my past would swirl into my mind: the way I used to caress my sewing machine, which was so obedient to my touch; the way Marigold Hurst had hugged me on the day of the scavenger hunt, as though she knew I would soon be Simon's wife; the kindness of Pet to me when I failed my French A level, saying in her soft Scottish voice, 'Dinna fret, girlie. Pet loves you. And life is long.'

It seemed to me at these moments that my past, in spite of the heartbreak I'd suffered, had been full of unexpected consolations and that my future, working as a secretary in a drab office, taking down dictation of stock phrases and then typing them up, would be quite devoid of them. But yet there was no other future. I would medicate my skin and go to work on the bus and then come home again and start drinking, or sometimes go down to the King's Road, looking for Julius Templeman or some other beautiful gazelle and then becoming their lousy fuck. It would be a life of boredom and shame.

And also I was broke. The bank refused to cash any more of my cheques. I lived for a couple of days on the last of my green apples and a box of Kraft Dairylea cheese triangles. I was so hungry I even had dreams of the old 'bacon pudding' at school. I finished off my last bottle of Chianti, then I phoned Daddy. He said, 'All right. I can't say I'm surprised. I'll put some money into your account, but you'll have to earn it off in the Christmas holidays and pay me back.'

'Earn it off how?' I asked.

'By working, Marianne. You know the meaning of that word "work", do you? Bartlett's will be taking on Christmas staff. I'll apply there on your behalf.'

Bartlett's was a department store in Newbury. It had been Bartlett's free paper bags we'd used to put our finds in on the day of the Hursts' scavenger hunt. Mummy went to Bartlett's at least once a week, to look for things she didn't know she needed but then quickly found that she did and put them on her account. Her cupboards were full of lacy bedjackets, silk underslips, boxes of bath cubes and suede gloves from Bartlett's. It wasn't a place where I ever imagined myself working, but now this was what awaited me when the term ended. I wondered for a moment if Mummy or Daddy would drive me the six miles into Newbury each morning, but quickly decided that of course they wouldn't want to do this. I was going to have to walk through the December snow and frost to the village of Weston Applegate and clamber on to a Green Line bus. And the sky would be dark. There would be no daylight. I would be too early for it in the winter dawns and too late for sunset in the afternoons.

I began work in the china department. Then the floor manager noticed how neatly I did up the parcels and transferred me to the gift-wrap desk. Here, I was expected to wear a little red Santa hat with a white bobble on it and greet the customers with an accommodating smile. Only rich people paid for gift wrap, people like the Fletcher-Blakes and the Pratts. I would be working with one other girl, called Paula Renton, from Reading. Paula Renton and I would display our selection of seasonal paper and our Hallmark ribbons in all their limitless shades and the customers would take their time choosing, but then want their gifts wrapped very fast, because they were of a class that disliked being made to wait for anything. But I didn't mind this work. Sometimes, I'd fashion quite complex bows or rosettes or suggest little unexpected swirls of glitter on the parcel. Paula said, 'That's quite a groovy touch, Marianne,' and I felt pleased. It was as if my skill at making clothes from *Vogue* patterns had been called upon here and people appreciated this and thanked me politely and never said that I'd failed or that they were in despair.

One day, when Paula was on her mid-morning break, a girl came up to the gift-wrap desk, holding a man's silk scarf in a shiny box. She looked at me and smiled as she put her parcel on my counter and I saw that it was Jasmine Hurst. I let out a little gasp. Jasmine said, 'I thought it was you, Marianne, but I wasn't sure. Your skin looks different.'

She was thirteen now and her long, springy hair had been cut and tamed. I said, 'I've never forgotten the scavenger hunt and the way you and Belinda rolled down Squirrels' Tump.' Jasmine said, 'Did you know Simon and Solange have got a little girl?' I said, 'Yes, so I heard.' Then Jasmine said, 'Did your mother tell you what name they chose?' and I said, 'No,' and Jasmine said, 'Well, I think it's a bit weird, but they've called her Marianne.'

There was a small queue forming behind Jasmine. I

took off my Santa hat because I just couldn't bear looking so ridiculous any more in front of Jasmine. I said to her, 'Choose your paper and ribbon and I'll do the present for you. Is the scarf for Simon?'

'Yes,' said Jasmine. 'He and Solange and Marianne are coming for Christmas, so I had to get everybody something expensive.'

'Quite right,' I said. I wanted to say other things, but I found I couldn't speak. I wanted to come out from behind the gift-wrap counter and hold Jasmine close to me and cry into her shoulder, but I knew I had to master myself somehow. I could see the floor manager standing by the Christmas-card display staring at me and then begin to mime 'Put on your Santa hat' and I didn't want to lose my job. Jasmine was staring at me, too, and her face had gone red and she suddenly blurted out, 'I think what's happened is all wrong! You were good fun, Marianne, and I thought Simon loved you.' Tears started rolling down her cheeks. The woman behind her in the gift-wrap queue coughed discreetly, as if to say, 'This is Bartlett's of Newbury, we can't have any kind of upset in here.' The floor manager came striding over and said, 'Is anything wrong, Miss Clifford? You know we're ultra-busy today?'

I shook my head. Speaking didn't seem to be something I could do at that moment. Jasmine pulled out a hankie and sobbed into that. The floor manager turned to the people waiting and said, 'Miss Clifford's colleague, Miss Renton, will be back from her coffee break in ten minutes. Perhaps you would like to come back then and she will wrap your gifts?' They went grumblingly away and when they'd moved off, the floor manager said sternly, 'Now, Miss Clifford . . .'

Jasmine said, 'It's not her fault. It's my fault. I don't need this present wrapped. I can do it myself.'

Jasmine took the box with Simon's silk scarf in it off the counter and said, 'I'm sorry, Marianne. I really am.' Then she turned and walked away and I watched her go, threading her way through Greetings Cards and Novelties and Christmas Fayre and I thought, I've never had a sister, but Jasmine was going to be my little sister-in-law and we would have played gin rummy together and turned cartwheels on the lawn and been as carefree as lambs.

'Well?' said the floor manager. 'What am I going to do about this? It is completely inexcusable. And you know you should be wearing your Santa hat at all times, so kindly put it on.'

I wasn't sacked that day. I worked right up to December the twenty-third, which was when my job officially ended, while Mummy prepared the kind of special food we never normally ate and Daddy took deliveries of wine and sherry. I bought a few presents, using my staff discount at Bartlett's. The only present I enjoyed buying was a ping-pong bat for Hugo Forster-Pellisier.

'The plan is,' Mummy had told me, 'we're going to have a quiet Christmas. Just a little drinks party to go to at the Hursts' tomorrow, where I suppose we're all meant to be drooling over Simon's *petite fille* – silly boy, what a waste of a good mind – and then on the twenty-ninth—'

'I'm not going to the Hursts' drinks party,' I said.

69

'Why not?' said Mummy.

'Because, as I told you years ago, I was in love with Simon Hurst and my heart has been broken ever since he got married. Why d'you think I failed most of my exams? Why do you imagine I've got acne?'

Mummy gaped at me. She was wrapping a pair of socks to give to Daddy and doing it badly. I took the parcel out of her hands and began to recut the wrapping paper to the proper size for the package. Mummy reached for a du Maurier cigarette and lit it and said, 'I really don't think it was love, was it? I think it was a schoolgirl crush, wasn't it?'

'No,' I said. 'It was love. Or rather, it *is* love. I'll always love Simon. Absolutely and forever.'

Mummy hated it when people said things to her that surprised or shocked her. She liked every conversation to jog along in a predictable way, as though it was an obedient dog trotting beside her on a taut lead. She sucked deeply on her cigarette, looking at me with a blank expression, and I could imagine her brain synapses in some kind of horrible tangle, undecided about which words to select for her to utter.

Eventually, she said, 'I'm sorry if we were too severe over the exams. Perhaps we should have been more understanding. But all you must do now is put the whole Simon thing out of your mind, Marianne.'

'Wrong,' I said. 'It's impossible to put it out of my mind. It was the most beautiful thing that's ever happened to me.'

Mummy got up and went to the window and looked out at the garden, where the fallen beech leaves were swirling around in the December wind. I could only guess at what she was feeling.

When Mummy and Daddy left for the Christmas drinks at the Hursts', I locked myself in my room, but once I was alone I began wondering whether Simon might have been hoping to see me and would be disappointed. I couldn't know whether this was the case or not and when Mummy and Daddy got back, breathing sherry fumes all over the place, I was determined not to ask them a single thing about the party. When we sat down to a dinner of baked ham with mashed potatoes and marmalade sauce – one of Mummy's peculiar seasonal specialities – they were both mainly silent and I was completely silent, so this was a strange Christmas Eve.

Towards the end of the meal, Daddy, whose nose had gone very scarlet, as though he were trying to morph into Rudolph the Red-Nosed Reindeer, picked up one of the crackers Mummy had put on the table and rattled it in my direction in a warning kind of way and you could hear the cheap little present bouncing around inside the cardboard tubing.

'I want you to pay attention to this,' he said. 'Mummy and I are agreed – we are absolutely agreed – that Simon Hurst has made a complete and utter mess of things.'

I could tell that he expected me to speak, so I said, 'Do you want to pull that cracker, Daddy?'

He shook his head. 'I want you to listen to me, Marianne. If Simon were my son,' he continued, 'I'm telling you that I would honestly—'

'He's not your son,' I said. 'You hardly know him. You have no right to criticise him.'

'Marianne,' said Mummy. 'Please don't shout at your father.'

'I'm not shouting,' I said. 'I just want to say that I don't believe you have any right to make pronouncements on what Simon has done or not done.'

'I think I have every right,' said Daddy, 'if what Mummy has told me about you and him is true. You wanted to get involved with him, didn't you?'

'I *was* "involved" with him.'

'All right, but luckily for you – and this is all I'm saying – you were far too young to contemplate anything serious, and now there he is, with a strange little French family he's trying to support by working in a bookshop. I mean, how much can that possibly earn him? If he hadn't flunked Oxford and been sent off to Paris—'

I put my hands over my ears and shouted, 'I don't want to hear about it! I don't want to hear about it!'

Daddy opened his mouth to say something else, but Mummy picked up her cracker and said quickly, 'She doesn't want to hear about it, Gerald. So let's all pull a cracker.'

'I don't agree,' said Daddy. 'I think she *should* hear about it.'

'She doesn't want to, darling. The best possible thing she can do is to forget all about it.'

'Well, I feel that she should see it as a warning – that lives can go wrong horribly early – and learn from it.'

'I'm sure she has learned from it.'

'Not well enough. If she doesn't work harder at that secretarial course—'

I stood up and pushed back my chair. I said, 'If you're going to talk about me as if I wasn't here, then I'm not going to be here.' Mummy and Daddy both gaped as I left the room. The thing I'd noticed about people their age was that when unexpected things happen to them, they are almost always lost for words, and then a small wave of pity for them breaks somewhere inside me and lingers for a short while.

On December the twenty-ninth, the Forster-Pellisiers came to stay with us for New Year. They arrived on a cold morning in their enormous car, which they called the Station Wagon. Everything the Forster-Pellisiers seemed to like was huge: the house in Cornwall with its gigantic garage, the luggage which accompanied them in the Station Wagon, the dog, Sparky. And now here was Hugo F-P, unseen by me since the holiday when we played table tennis wearing fur coats, grown to an astounding height, towering over Daddy and looking down at me as though he might have been a giant figure on a billboard.

'How are you, Yeti?' he said.

He'd grown his red hair long, as if trying to be a King's Road gazelle, but the rest of him was clothed in tweed, so the curls draped over his collar just looked a bit embarrassing.

'I see you've grown, Anthracite,' I said.

'Yes,' he said. 'Can't seem to stop. What about you?'

'Nope. Haven't grown at all. My life stopped when I was sixteen. Just acquired acne, that's all. Gift from God.'

Hugo smiled. And I remembered that this was a thing I liked about him, his kind smile.

Mr and Mrs Forster-Pellisier – or Jocelyn and Felicity, as I remembered I had to call them – heaved their huge suitcases from the Station Wagon and left them standing on the gravel near the white columns, for Hugo to carry upstairs. Felicity said, 'There you are, Hugo. That's the price you pay for being so large and strong,' and Mummy and Daddy and Jocelyn and Felicity disappeared into the warm house, while Hugo and I and the luggage just stood waiting in the freezing December air and the dog Sparky ran in circles all around the lawn, pissing here and there as he went. Hugo turned to me and said, 'I've taken up riding quite seriously since I last saw you. I've got a friend who's lending me a horse for the point-to-point on Saturday. Will you come and cheer me on?'

'You mean there's a horse tall enough for you, Anthracite?'

'Yes, there is. Brilliant steeplechaser. Named Midnight Sun. I stand a chance of winning. You could put half a crown on me.'

'Absolutely,' I said. 'My bets on life quite often fail, but I don't mind betting on a horse race.'

'What d'you mean, your bets on life quite often fail?'

'Oh, I just make the wrong decisions about what's going to happen.'

Hugo took his gaze away from Sparky – who had wearied of mundane urinating and was now very studiously engaged in more interesting crapping in one of Mummy's rose beds – and looked down at me from his impressive height and I saw that his look was tender. 'You know something, Yeti?' he said.

'Know what?'

'I'm really glad to see you.'

'Oh,' I said. 'That's nice. Normally people aren't.'

'Aren't what?'

'Glad to see me. I don't seem to have any friends at the secretarial school.'

'Why not?'

'They know I don't take it seriously, and they do. They want to spend their lives taking down dictation, and I . . . well, I don't know what I want to do. I think I might prefer to die.'

Hugo said, 'Really?'

'I don't know. The trouble about dying is that the means to bring it about seem a bit hard to arrange.'

'If you died, Yeti, we could never go surfing again.'

'True,' I said. And I remembered how thrilling it had been to ride the waves and be thrown into the beach and how we'd kept going back beyond the breakers to begin the process all over again until we were exhausted and lay down on the sand like runners at the end of a long race.

I said, on sudden impulse, 'Let's carry the luggage up to your rooms and then take Sparky for a walk. I'd rather walk than drink sherry, wouldn't you?'

'Yes. But won't you be cold?'

'No. I was really cold one night in London. I was

kicked out of a guy's bed and I tried to walk home and a fog came down, the kind of fog Dickens writes about, and the cars looked like mounds of hay and I was so confused and freezing, I might as well have been halfway up Everest without a guide.'

'Whose bed were you kicked out of?'

'Oh, he was a photographer. He had long hair, like yours, only not that colour. He picked me up in a coffee bar called the Picasso. He reminded me of an antelope.'

'An antelope.'

'Yes. You know: treading very softly about the world. And aware of his own beauty.'

'Do you sleep with lots of guys?'

'Not lots. Why d'you ask, Anthracite?'

'Only because, if you do, I might like to be one of them.'

The suitcases were all identical, coloured red and marked *Revelation*. I wondered for a moment what they actually revealed. They were so heavy, I wondered if the Forster-Pellisiers had decided to stay with us until springtime. We set them down gently in the guest rooms and I grabbed one of Daddy's old coats from the pegs by the back door and Hugo and I went out into the drive and then along the lane that led to some stately woods of oak and beech where, even in winter, you always heard birds calling. The coat I'd chosen came down almost to my ankles and I said to Hugo that I liked the way it made me look like a derelict person, which was how I felt myself to be, and he said, 'Well, yes, or like a yeti, which is who you actually are.'

Hugo had put Sparky on the lead, but he was one of those dogs who tugged on this all the while, longing to run free, so I said, 'Let him go. He can chase rabbits. He'll be in heaven.'

He went bounding off, a streak of black and white among the grey stems of trees, and I thought how marvellous it might be to be a dog, with no need to earn a living or worry about your skin or listen to all the heartless things your parents said.

To make polite conversation as we walked, Hugo asked me about the secretarial college and I told him how much I hated it and how, in the typing lessons, with the din of fifteen Remingtons hammering at my head, I sometimes felt my mind straying into madness.

He said, 'It'd be a shame if you went mad, Yeti. In my view, you're a much stronger person than you think you are.'

'How do you know that?' I said.

'I don't *know* it. I just think it's probably true. You now have to decide what your direction is going to be.'

'I don't have a direction. I had one long ago and then it was snatched away from me and now I'm in limbo. I'd prefer to be a dog. Or preferably a horse. What about you, Anthracite?'

Hugo didn't answer. He looked up at the sky, the filigree of it we could see through the denuded tree branches, then he stopped walking and stared all around him at the silent trees. He said, 'These are lovely woods. I miss Berkshire. Do you?'

'I don't know,' I said. 'I think I just miss being fifteen

when everything seemed beautiful. But I don't really want to talk about my life. Tell me about yours.'

Anthracite had done well at his A levels and had been taken on at Sotheby's salerooms to learn about the value of art and antiques. He said he was in the humble position of a porter but reassured me that the word 'porter' at Sotheby's not only meant that he helped to physically move objects from one branch of the auction house in St George Street to the other branch in New Bond Street, but in fact denoted somebody who was predicted to learn quickly how to number and date paintings and furniture.

'Is that what you want to do?' I asked. 'Number and date things?'

'Yes. Only by doing that do you learn about value.'

'What do you mean exactly, Anthrax?'

'What did you call me?'

'Anthrax. My vocal cords get cold saying three-syllable names in winter weather.'

'Anthrax is a deadly disease.'

'Is it? I thought it was a skin medication and you could touch my face and cure it. Tell me what you mean by "learning about value".'

Hugo smiled the sort of resigned smile that the parents of very young children have on their faces for most of their waking hours. Then he said, 'Well, I'm learning to look at things and price them. It involves studying what they actually are.'

'I see,' I said. 'So what "things", for instance?'

'Right. Well, the other day I was shown a Louis XIV-style

ebony and brass marquetry vitrine and an eighteenth-century bentside spinet – and told to price them.'

'And?'

'I was way off. I overpriced the vitrine and I under-priced the spinet by miles. But this is my apprenticeship. I'm enjoying learning.'

I said I thought this sounded bizarre but somehow OK. I looked at Hugo and imagined his head filling up with arcane knowledge under his orange curls. I remembered how we'd picked our way through all the *stuff* in the garage in the rented house in Cornwall and how this had preoccupied us for hours and I wondered if he'd thought then that discovering random things, like old croquet mallets and broken deckchairs, and then progressing through time to ebony and brass marquetry vitrines, was what would see him through his life and keep him from despair.

It was cold on the day of the point-to-point, but freezing conditions have never put Mummy off organising picnics. I think she must have had some beautiful picnics in her past somewhere, perhaps provided by her elegant mother, my dead grandmother, Violet, and the memory of these kept her warm and optimistic.

She put down an old rug on the rough grass beside the F-Ps' Station Wagon, a little sheltered from the wind by the open door of the car, and we all huddled onto this and drank sloe gin, followed by a picnic of hard-boiled eggs, cold chicken and radishes. Mummy produced salt in a little twist of paper to go with the radishes and I could tell how proud she was of this thoughtful addition to our meal by the smile on her face as she brought it out, which was like the smile on the face of a conjuror perfecting a difficult trick. She annoyed me so much that I said, 'Shame you forgot to make any mayonnaise, Mummy. I'm sure Granny Violet wouldn't have deigned to eat cold chicken without mayonnaise,' but she pretended not to hear this and Hugo whispered, 'Don't be beastly, Yeti,' though I could tell that he somehow understood what I was feeling.

Underneath his tweed overcoat, Hugo was wearing jockey's silks. The colours of the silks were purple and green with a white star on the back of the shirt and everything was a bit too small for Hugo's tall frame, so that it looked creased in the wrong places and the star was pulled so taut it almost didn't look like a star any more, but like a star*fish* with bendy limbs. But his boots were stupendous, huge and strong and gleaming, and this gave me confidence that he might be able to win his race. When I looked at him, taking tiny sips of sloe gin, staying calm in the face of his coming ride over huge brushwood fences, I had the thought that he might be a courageous person, through and through, and that without any fuss, he would probably have a decent life and never stand in Hyde Park wishing telephone boxes were euthanasia booths. I envied him, but I also admired him a bit and when he got up to go and find his horse, before we'd finished eating the radishes, I said, 'I'm coming with you, Anthracite. I'm going to help you saddle up.'

His horse, Midnight Sun, reminded me of Merlin the

stallion Pet had ridden in our races round the old riding-school field: sleek and huge with an agitated look in its eye. I told Hugo that riding had been the only thing I'd been good at in my teen years and that the smell of horses was probably as comforting to me as the scent of Je Reviens was to Mummy, and he said, 'Good for you, Yeti, so help me here – hold the bridle very close to his mouth, while the saddle goes on. All right? Try not to let him move his head too much.'

We were in some old barns smelling of dry straw and dung, in a distant part of the point-to-point course. You could look over to where the cars were all parked and see the winter sun shining on them and imagine the picnic hampers being hauled out of them and all the people pretending they weren't cold, and I was glad to be here, with the horses – the fret and beauty of them and the sense of something colossal about to happen.

Not far from the car park, there was a rectangular bit of grass designated as the paddock, where the horses walked round and round for a while so that the racegoers could assess them before they placed their bets. Hugo's friend Jason, the owner of Midnight Sun, had brought along a stable boy, who was going to lead the stallion round the paddock. I wanted to say to Jason, 'Let me do it. I can lead him round and help to calm him,' but as if reading my thoughts, Hugo said, 'Will you come and stand with me, Yeti, and we can talk about ping-pong or something while I'm waiting for the off?' I said I would and I told him that I had some chewing gum in my pocket which was very beneficial to the nerves and he thanked me and took the piece of gum I offered and suddenly said, 'Do you remember that kiss we had in Cornwall? I thought I'd forget all about it, but somehow I didn't.' Then he put the chewing gum in his mouth and strode on ahead of me, as though he didn't want an answer or almost as though he hadn't asked a question at all, so I just kept quiet and followed him to the paddock.

Felicity and Jocelyn Forster-Pellisier were already there, looking cold now that they were no longer sheltered by the Station Wagon, and they both put an arm around Hugo, one each side of him, like they were posing for a family photograph. I hadn't liked them much in Cornwall, but now I seemed to get a glimpse of how much they loved Hugo and how the thought of all the high fences he was about to jump probably made their blood begin to freeze, and I thought that in their hearts they were probably rather decent in a rich and snobbish sort of way.

We all stood watching as the stable boy led Midnight Sun round and round and saw how he kept tossing his head and it was then that I first asked myself the question 'How much can horses think?' When they see crowds of people wearing Barbours and wellingtons and smelling of sloe gin, do they know there's going to be a race in which they might die? Do they know about dying? Do they long to be put back in the trailer and taken to the quiet field where they're just allowed to graze and swish their tails and lie down in the sun? When Mirabelle and Merlin saw me and Pet, did they think, Aha, here are the good riders and this is promising, because sooner or later we're going to have a wild gallop and all the trees will be cheering?

I was going to ask Hugo what his opinion was on the subject of horse consciousness, but now it was time for him to saddle up. The stable boy held Midnight Sun very close to the bit while Hugo shortened the stirrups. After this adjustment, the stirrups looked too short for his long legs, but in fact when he got on the horse, the extreme bend of his knees ensured that his immaculate boots just slotted his feet into place, and I thought, Old Anthracite clearly knows a thing or two about this, and people *knowing stuff* – like Simon knew so much about Jean-Paul Sartre and nihilism – is always to be praised. So Hugo went up in my estimation and I thought how grisly it would be if he died on this cold day in December 1963.

To watch the race, I went to stand with Felicity and Jocelyn at the last fence. There was a long run-in to this after the final bend in the course and Felicity said, 'Watch carefully when they round that corner, Marianne. You may think at this point that the leading horse has it in the bag, but they're tiring by now and they still have the last fence to jump and the rising ground to the finish, so there's a double excitement.'

I said, 'Thank you, Felicity. Now I understand the lie of the land.'

Then Mummy and Daddy appeared. Daddy's face was quite puce and stupid-looking from the gin, and Mummy was complaining that the lumpy grass hurt her ankles, and I thought they probably didn't care a jot whether Anthracite survived the race, and this led me to

83

wonder what it was they *did* care about in life, apart from games of Scrabble and collecting blue-and-white china, and inheriting Granny Violet's valuable emerald choker. So my thoughts were all tumbling over each other as the race began, but as it progressed and we strained to see over to the other side of the course and the tumult of the horses' hooves got louder, I found myself going into a kind of silent trance, like I'd switched everything and everyone off and all that was left was that long run-in and then the final jump and the last dash to the winning post.

The horses were at the penultimate fence now and I could see, in the flash of purple and green, that Hugo was among the leading three and as they appeared round the final corner, I began shouting, 'Come on, Midnight Sun!' And Felicity and Jocelyn joined in and I hoped Anthracite could hear us all yelling like the *demos* of ancient Rome yelled for their favourite gladiator, but because I was still in my trance, I wasn't sure, in fact, whether we were actually shouting or making no sound at all.

And as Midnight Sun leapt over the last hurdle, I thought, I know what the silence in my head is: it's an absence, titled 'Simon'. For the whole of the last minute, I haven't thought about him. And I realised that the thrill of the race had pushed him aside, and it had been peaceful there, just for a moment, without him, and I knew that I would do almost anything to send him far away from me and stay in this quiet state.

I leaned over the flimsy rail, still shouting for Midnight Sun, and I let all the noise of the world come roaring back, with its danger and its striving, and I saw clods of turf flying up behind the horses' hooves and I thought how magnificent this was – the earth itself being torn up and hanging for a tiny second in the cold blue of the December sky before falling back onto this field in Berkshire. And then I saw Hugo start whipping the flanks of Midnight Sun and when it felt the whip, the horse knew what was being asked of it and its agitated eyes looked white and terrible as it came surging on. And I felt a wonderful joy for it and for Anthracite as they passed the winning post.

III

I married Hugo Forster-Pellisier a year later. I was twenty and Hugo was twenty-two.

It was snowing on the wedding day and all the cars slithered around on the icy lanes and the guests stood stiffly in their church pews, looking pale with terror. Daddy had been furious that we'd chosen to have a winter wedding. He'd said to Mummy, 'Even in war, Lal, one does one's best not to have to contend with the weather. Remember the Ardennes.' And Mummy had had to say to him, 'Gerald darling, don't be naïve. They've got to marry quickly because Marianne is preggers,' and Daddy had said, 'Oh Christ. Is there no end to what that child gets wrong?'

Pregnant or not, I almost didn't get married. On the morning of the wedding, I sat on my single bed in my room at Hastings House and thought, I've just had my very last night in this bed, where all the dreams of my future with Simon were dreamed. And this made me feel so sad and helpless that I put a pillow over my face and cried into it and I began to wonder if I wouldn't just pack a small suitcase and walk to Weston Applegate and wait for a Green Line bus and then board the bus and disappear by getting on a train at Newbury station, a train to Wales or some other place where Mummy and Daddy and Hugo would never find me, and climb into the snows of some savage hill and wait for death.

But then Pet came into my room and saw me howling into the pillow and said, 'Och, for the Lord's sake, Marianne . . .'

Pet was now a student at the brand-new University of Essex, studying sociology. I'd had to ask her what sociology actually was and she'd said, 'Well, it's a study of how things are and how they were and how they might ideally become in human society,' and I'd said, 'What things?' and Pet had said, 'Everything,' and I'd said, 'You mean your course is a Study of Everything?' and she'd said, 'Pretty much everything, including, it seems, the things you thought you knew already, except that you discover that you didn't know them well enough, or you knew them in a wrong kind of way, or your interpretation of them was morally and intellectually flawed.' So I was left feeling confused.

Pet had stayed the night before at Hastings House as she was going to be my maid of honour. I'd refused to have bridesmaids as I knew I'd have to choose Rowena Fletcher-Blake and Cordelia Pratt and I just didn't love these girls any more; the only friend I still loved was Pet and so she and I had gone to Dickins & Jones together and chosen her dress, which was copper-coloured with silver embroidery trim, and we bought a sort of bagel of fake flowers for her fantastic hair. When Mummy and

Daddy had been introduced to Pet, I'd understood straight away that they didn't like her; she was too Scottish and blunt and clever and enormous for them. But I didn't care.

Now Pet knelt down by me and stroked my arm and said, 'I'm guessing it's the old Simon heartbreak, is it?'

I was crying too hard to reply, so Pet just kept stroking me and said, 'I so completely understand it, Marianne. You asked me what sociologists do and this is it: they understand things and how they've come about and try to suggest ways of putting them right. So if you want me to go downstairs and tell your parents that you can't marry Hugo, that's what I'll do. But you have to be sure. OK? You have to say to me, "I am absolutely sure that I don't want to get married today. I don't want to become Mrs Hugo Forster-Pellisier." Then I'll let everybody know. Are you hearing me, girlie? I will do this for you, but only if you're one hundred per cent sure.'

I took the pillow off my face and looked down at Pet, who was wearing the same pyjamas she'd worn at Crowbourne House School, and when I saw this old faded and frayed nightwear, the sight of it made me want to put my arms around her and cry for all eternity. I said, 'I wish I was a horse.'

This made Pet smile and she said, 'I have the same thought from time to time. Beautiful meadows. Oats in a bucket. Eh? But right now, there is a human decision to be made. Isn't there?'

Pet climbed up onto the bed and I let myself fall against her and she held me very tightly and the snot from my crying soaked into her ragged pyjama top, and I thought how if this had been Rowena she would have pulled away and said, 'Yuck, Marianne, now my shoulder's all slimy,' but Pet just rocked me very gently, like you might rock a child who's woken from a nightmare. Then she said, 'What you might have to do, you know, is to think far beyond today, way beyond this wedding and the ceremony of it, to the time when you have your baby. Because – listen to me, Marianne . . . cease your lamentation and listen to me – I've heard it said that when young women have babies, their love for them just takes over their hearts and preoccupies them night and day, and when you feel this kind of love, I reckon you're going to be happy about it. I really think you will be. I do. And if I'm going to be the godmother, like you so darlingly suggested, we could take the baby to Scotland and feed her haggis-flavoured baby food, while we get a bit tippled on Scotch whisky. How about that for a plan?'

I stopped crying and said, 'Do they make haggis-flavoured baby food?' And Pet said she was pretty sure they did and once the baby was through that phase and on to grown-up haggis, then she might look around at the complicated world and be glad she had a red-haired, Scottish-looking daddy.

'Just a thought,' she added.

So then, later that day, I was standing at the altar with Hugo. He was exactly eleven inches taller than me, so I had to look up at him when we said our vows and I wondered if my borrowed tiara was going to fall backwards off my head and clatter onto the cold stone of the church floor. I saw that Hugo's face was all creased up in a sort of hectic smile, the kind of smile you try to put on when you know you might cry, and I thought, I was right about old Anthracite, he's a very decent, honest and kind man and part of me is truly grateful for this.

There was a reception at Hastings House. It had had to be arranged with what Mummy called 'indecent haste', but she'd managed to cajole some caterers into making beef Wellington for fifty people and to order a quantity of gilt chairs and flimsy tables covered with white linen tablecloths. These were all crowded into a marquee on the back lawn, where Daddy and I had played cricket when I was a child (impersonating the son-he'd-never-had) and the waiters squeezed and squirmed their way between them, holding aloft the platters of Wellington and pouring champagne. Electric heaters had been rigged up in the marquee and, for some reason, I was troubled by these and kept imagining them setting fire to the drapery of the tent and all of us going up in angry flames, like the girl, Harriet, who plays with matches in Heinrich Hoffman's *Struwwelpeter* and burns to death, wearing a green dress.

Also, it began to snow outside, a regular blizzard of snow, so then I thought, Suppose the roads are impassable and we're all stuck inside this marquee for days and nights? This thought made me very anxious and I just longed for all this to be over and to be in a quiet hotel room with Anthracite and feel the comfort of what he called his 'todger' (a homely kind of word) inside me.

93

This todger, like the rest of him, was rather large and this largeness I'd always found surprising and quite exciting. It was what Mummy might have called 'a key factor' in my willingness to keep going to bed with Hugo . . . to keep on and on going to bed with him, after the rapture of his win at the point-to-point, until it was too late to tell him that I didn't totally love him, because I was going to have his child. And I kept wondering, had it been just like this for Simon: that there had been some uniquely exciting or comforting thing about making love to Solange and so he kept on doing this without thinking much about it – until she was pregnant and he had to marry her?

When Hugo got up to make his speech at the reception, with the snow pelting down outside the plastic windows of the marquee and the wind sighing in all its fragile, flammable corners, I had no idea what he was going to say. Pet was sitting next to me, with the flower bagel still adorning her hair, and I clutched her hand under the table and she whispered, 'Why are you shivering?' And I said, 'I just don't like the way the snow's falling,' and she said, 'It'll be dark soon and you won't see it.'

Hugo had written his speech on minute little bits of paper, which he produced from the pocket of his trousers. The paper was all crumpled and I worried that the speech was going to be some stuttering sort of fiasco, but Anthracite smoothed out the creases in his notes and stood very tall, like he was already a senior auctioneer at Sotheby's, and all the guests went quiet and turned their faces towards him, like sunflowers towards the sun.

He began to talk about the meaning of the words 'heart's desire'. He said that when he met me in Cornwall and we'd played table tennis together, he knew that his heart had begun talking to him. He said, 'If I remember rightly, I won most of the ping-pong games, even though Marianne had some snappy shots, but I wasn't yet happy because what I hadn't won and what I didn't win for my poor old yearning heart for a long time was the love of Marianne Clifford. But now I have won it. I truly believe I have. I've got my heart's desire. I love you, Marianne. I love you, my sweet wife. I will love you forever. And this is all that matters. This is all I want to say.'

On my left, I heard Pet whisper to herself, 'What a touching fandango,' and then everybody began clapping and I looked along at Daddy, whose face was as pink and shiny as a crab apple above the Irish Guards dress uniform he'd insisted on wearing, and I could tell that, almost for the first time in my life, he was proud of me, because he saw that I had been capable of inspiring a good man's love.

A hired Bentley with a chauffeur in a peaked cap, paid for by Daddy, drove us very slowly and carefully to London through the blizzard. I felt sorry for this chauffeur, whose name was Mr Fratelli and who surely belonged in some warmer country. I said to him, 'I've never been to Sardinia or anywhere with a name like that, but I've heard that those places are wonderful.' And when I said this, I suddenly thought, Now I sound exactly like Mummy; I have entered the first act of a tragedy titled *Becoming Lal*.

Hugo and I sat in the back under a rug and somewhere east of Slough, I fell asleep with drunken exhaustion. When I woke up, I felt sick and I had to ask Mr Fratelli to stop the Bentley so that I could struggle out of it and puke on the roadside. The snow had stopped falling but the air was so cold, it seemed to turn everything purple. When I got back into the warm car and Hugo gave me a clean hankie, I said, 'How are we going to exist in a totally purple world?'

Mr Fratelli deposited us at the Berkeley Hotel, then in its old location on the corner of Berkeley Street. I congratulated this kind Italian man on driving so bravely. I had no idea what time it was, but I felt a ravening hunger and when we were shown to our room, I said to the bellboy, 'Is there some means of obtaining cheese on toast and a mug of hot cocoa?'

Our room was on the second floor, on the Piccadilly side of the hotel, and when you looked down, all you could see were the tops of buses choking the street and people trying to scurry between them towards the drab-looking curtained windows of the Ritz, and I said to Hugo, 'I don't remember how our honeymoon got put into this place, do you?'

He reminded me that we'd looked at brochures of Sardinia, but that the travel agent had told us that even Sardinia was cold in December and we would have to go 'to the other side of the world' to find the sun, and this would be too expensive for an apprentice valuer at Sotheby's. I had been going to say that perhaps Daddy would have paid, but then I'd remembered the fuss

Daddy had made about the price of the gilt chairs and the beef Wellington and how Mummy had said to me, 'Don't expect much more from us after this, darling. Daddy's worried that the army pension's not keeping up.'

Now I said to Hugo, 'Do you wish we were on a beach in Zambia?' and Hugo said, 'There are no beaches in Zambia, Yeti. It's a land-locked country.'

I looked down again at the buses and the frantic little people in Piccadilly and I thought, I wonder what's wrong with me that I know so little about the world, and the embarrassment and sadness of this choked me for a moment and I said, 'I don't think I'm going to be able to be a good mother, do you, Anthracite? I just don't know enough about anything. How on earth am I going to cope?'

Hugo had lain down on the big bed, with its shiny cover. He beckoned me over to him. He said, 'Stop fretting about everything, Marianne. This is our wedding night.'

I said, 'It's not night yet, is it? It may be dark, but the red buses are still all crammed up together in Piccadilly in a daytime kind of way. And I can't take care of the todger, Hugo, till I've had some cocoa.'

Before I married Hugo, I'd finished the secretarial course and started applying for secretarial jobs. The very word 'secretarial' sent little wavelets of despair into my heart. I stared at the certificate the college had given me, with my name on it, *Miss Marianne Clifford*, in careful italic writing, and felt that it was something I didn't care to own. But

Mummy said it was the 'passport' to my future and that the time had now come to 'stand on your own two feet'.

I said, 'All right. But which shoes do you suggest?' and Mummy said, 'That you try to make jokes about serious things, Marianne, has never served you well in any of your endeavours, as you should have understood by now. And if you think it amuses me, you're wrong. It has never amused me and it never will.' I nevertheless looked down at my feet, which are narrow and elegant, with the toes very perfectly aligned, like little peach-coloured beans in a pod, and I thought, It's a shame nobody has ever remarked on their beauty. I wondered for a moment if I couldn't bypass secretarial work and get a job modelling sandals, but then I saw that this was just another of my inappropriate thoughts.

While waiting to hear about job applications, I went to visit Pet at Essex University. She was lodged in a high grey tower and had to share a kitchen with thirteen other people, but she was breathless with excitement at her student life. She had a new group of friends. They all called her Petronella, not Pet, and she seemed to like this rediscovery of her true name. Most of them had bodies as pale and skinny as leeks, but Pet said, 'In fact, they're not people who can be bent or plucked; they're really angry.' She told me that their aim was to rise up against privilege and all the decades-long unfairnesses in British society and usher in a new age of social equality. When Pet said, 'I don't suppose you've ever thought about any of this, Marianne, have you?' I replied that when I'd worked on Bartlett's gift-wrap desk, I had understood that only a certain class of customer could afford to have their gifts professionally wrapped by me and that I had had moments of thinking this wasn't quite right. And Pet roared with mirth.

We went to an Indian restaurant with two of Pet's new friends, a boy called Orlando, who reminded me a little of Julius Templeman, and a girl called Savannah, who had beautiful, narrow hands adorned with bands of silver and a throaty voice. Through the harsh lighting in the restaurant, Orlando and Savannah smoked roll-ups and stared at my acne and I could feel them recoil from me before I'd had a chance to say anything at all. Pet saw this too and after we'd ordered a lot of unfamiliar food, she began to tell them what a loyal friend I'd been to her at school and how we'd gone riding together and galloped 'like Arabs' around a field of clover.

'You can't say "like Arabs", Petronella,' said Orlando. 'That's such insulting, racist language'.

'Och, fuck off, Orlando,' said Pet. 'Everybody knows about Arabian horses and their fearless riders. That was all I meant.'

'I know,' said Orlando. 'But you just can't say things like that any more.'

So then Pet and Orlando and Savannah began a big conversation about how people betrayed themselves by certain names and phrases they used, and I kept completely silent for a long time while little metal bowls of curry and lentils and coconut-flavoured rice were set down before us. I didn't feel much like eating any of this. I wanted to say that prejudice wasn't found only in language; that Orlando and Savannah had made their judgement about me on the basis of my bad skin and my posh voice, and that if they bothered to get to know me, they might have understood that I was a brave and fearless rider, that I had once been lovable enough to steal the heart of the most beautiful boy in Berkshire and wild enough to lose my virginity in the back of a Morris Minor, wearing a home-made taffeta frock, but it seemed easier to keep silent. I didn't want to say anything that would embarrass Pet.

After the meal, as we made the long trek in the dark through the outskirts of Colchester to Pet's tower block, and Orlando and Savannah peeled off down some terrifying-looking cul-de-sac to visit a club, Pet said, 'So where are you now in your life, Marianne? D'you still feel lost?'

But I found that I couldn't answer her. I just took her hand and felt the familiar warmth of it and we walked on under the sodium lights, with the traffic surging by. After a while, I said, 'I wish we were in Scotland, in a place you knew, living in a bothy, miles from every human habitation.'

The job I found was on a women's magazine, doing secretarial work for an agony aunt who called herself Liliane Hart. The offices were in Farringdon Street. I occupied a corner of the large room, with a thin window giving me a sliver of a glance towards Fleet Street. I was positioned in front of an enormous Adler typewriter, and for some reason I couldn't exactly name, this machine, with its heavy carriage, its German name and its emphatic-sounding keys, brought a bit of cheer into my mind.

Also, the letters we got from readers were completely absorbing in a macabre kind of way. They reminded me that England was densely populated with unhappy people, mainly of the female gender. When I walked down the King's Road, or tottered on platform heels towards Biba like everyone else that season, I'd always got the feeling that everybody I set eyes on was living a marvellous life, but now, in Farringdon Street, I understood that there was this other race of women so vexed and confused by the existence they found themselves in that they decided to believe in the benevolence of Liliane Hart, like children believe in the benevolence of Father Christmas. They went out and bought a pad of Basildon Bond notepaper and a Bic biro and wrote down their sorrows and waited for Liliane Hart to give them the answers to the questions that kept them from their sleep.

Most of these questions were about abandonment and/or male violence. One of these was from a woman who had gone to a bowling alley with a chap from Margate and he'd suddenly said to her that when he rolled his weighted ball, he sometimes imagined that the skittles it was going to topple were tiny little naked women, and that gave him a thrill like no other. She asked in her letter if we thought she should stay with this man or not, and we advised her to pack her bags as soon as she'd checked out the train timetables from Margate to anywhere. Another was from a married woman who had left her husband to live with an airline pilot in Manchester and the airline pilot had taken her to the Midland Hotel for cocktails, told her he was going out to buy a box of matches and never came back. She said to us: *I am ashamed of myself for leaving a perfectly good husband for a man with no moral integrity and yet I long to get him back. What should I do?* I said to Liliane Hart, 'It could be that she was just seduced by the pilot's uniform, which is almost comprehensible, and it could also be that the airline seducer was already married to someone else and so experienced a sudden wave of remorse. Perhaps we should think about this one some more before replying.'

Liliane Hart, whose real name was Janice Ludlow, was a starchy woman in her fifties with permed hair and an adoration of Vera Lynn, who had told me at my job interview that Dame Vera had 'got everybody through the war, single-handed'. The thing that had got me this job as her secretarial assistant was my saying in reply to this: 'I know my parents would agree, Miss Ludlow, but my father, who was a colonel in the Irish Guards, also made a contribution and almost lost his life in Germany.'

'Ah, well, yes, of course. Your father was a soldier,' said Liliane Hart. 'Such bravery. Such loss. Such endurance. How marvellous. I wonder if you can start next Monday?'

I'd begun my affair with Hugo by this time and when I told him I'd got this job on the magazine, he took me out to dinner at the Bistro Vino and we slugged our way through two bottles of Chianti and returned to Hugo's flat in Kensington and made love lying on a kilim rug from Habitat, and I think it was that night, or somewhere around that time, that Hugo first told me that he loved me and I said, 'No, no, Anthracite. Absolutely not. It's just a little crush on me that you've manufactured.' He looked incredibly hurt when I said this. His damp orange hair hung down like seaweed around his sorrowing face. He folded the todger away in his trousers and zipped it up with a kind of finality. Then he crawled off to the bedroom and closed the door and I went to sleep on the rug. I knew I should be feeling bad about hurting Hugo, in just the same way that Mummy had hurt me, with her ignorant remark about a 'crush', but somehow I was too tired to think about it.

The magazine gave me a week off for my wedding. When I told Janice Ludlow, who was a single woman, that I was getting married, she looked both surprised and hurt. She reminded me that we still hadn't replied to the woman from Manchester with her faithless airline pilot and then asked me if I didn't think I was too young 'for matrimony' and I said that no, I had decided on this particular future at the age of fifteen. What I didn't say was that the person I had been planning to marry then wasn't the person I was marrying now, but remembering this, I had a sudden and fierce memory of sitting on the top of Squirrels' Tump with Simon, on the day of Jasmine's scavenger hunt, with all our beautiful lives to come spread out at our feet. And I wanted to confess to Liliane Hart, there and then, that my heart had been broken and however hard I tried, I didn't seem able to mend it. I had been left in a metaphorical Midland Hotel crying into a cocktail glass. I wanted to say, 'I may more or less look like somebody with an OK life, but inside me I'm a ruin.'

I was also a pregnant ruin, but I didn't tell Janice this until later. I'd become quite fond of my Adler and my comfy office chair and my thin window, from which I sometimes fancied I could hear the roar of the Fleet Street printing machines, capturing the news from all across the globe. I liked the proximity of this, as if I – who was in reality nobody – could somehow be included in World Affairs, and I didn't want to lose this job. My secretarial duties weren't too humiliating. Janice Ludlow dictated letters in a hesitant kind of way, giving my Gregg's short-hand time to loop it all down, and right from the start she consulted me about the great variety of sad and perplex-ing things the readers wrote about. She told me one day that I was 'wise for my years', which was a thing abso-lutely nobody had ever thought or said about me ever before, including myself. I said that I didn't believe I was wise at all and that clearly Pet's friends at Essex had considered me an imbecile, but the one thing I was – perhaps – able to understand was human pain. When I said this, Janice Ludlow patted her permed hair and then wiped a tear from her spinster's eye.

More and more, I became the person who suggested how we should reply to our weekly deluge of letters. I said to Janice, 'I don't think we're able to solve problems, really, are we? But we can just sort of put the readers in a state of mind where they can experience moments of new happiness,' and she agreed. We sometimes stooped to reminding desperate people about the Beauty of Eng-land, as told to me by the mistresses of Crowbourne House School, or the faithfulness of dogs, or – also at my suggestion – the psychic wonder of going surfing in huge Cornish breakers. I quickly understood that Janice Ludlow, aka Liliane Hart, was no better and no worse than anybody with an ounce of human empathy at suggesting the means by which unhappiness can be overcome.

Not surprisingly, doing this job day after day, I fell into a pattern of self-questioning about my own state of mind. It was like I wrote a daily letter to Liliane Hart, asking her to tell me if, by getting pregnant and then deciding to marry Hugo, I was now out of the zone in which sadness for my lost life with Simon could still slay me with a deadly wound. Except, I never confided in Janice about my past. In fact, now that I hardly ever saw Pet, who was lately very taken up with the CND movement, I just didn't talk about it to anybody. But, as time went on, instead of being able to put my heart into cold storage, I began to obsess more and more about Solange.

I'd never seen Solange and I'd avoided asking people who'd met her any questions about her. Part of me hoped she might be ugly, with sallow skin and fatty legs. I'd imagine Simon walking down a Paris boulevard with this person and their little girl, Marianne, and for some reason, I arranged them all in a strung-out kind of line. Marianne went skipping ahead, with her brown hair like Simon's bouncing on sweet little skinny shoulders. Then came Simon, sauntering along, tall and aloof but with an affectionate eye on his daughter. And then poor old Solange came trudging into view. She was always loaded down with shopping, or perhaps not with shopping, but with the weight of something or other, which might have been an actual thing or just the weight of her disappointment in Simon, who no longer made love to her, who was trying and failing to write a novel, and who was still stuck in his job at the bookstore, earning some stressful low wage . . .

But then when I'd made this composite picture, I remembered that it might not be accurate at all. Solange might be a beauty. Her ankles might be as slim as cuttlefish bones. She might be superbly schooled in the thoughts of Simone de Beauvoir. She might be able to produce home-made mayonnaise with the merest twirl of her beautiful, tanned arms. In bed, she might have sexual tricks that had never entered my consciousness. And she might be a marvellous mother, binding Marianne and Simon to her forever.

It's strange how patterns of thought perform a repeating dance, like the pattern of the William Morris wallpaper in our hall, which just ran into itself and started all over again. My preoccupation with Solange was like that wallpaper, running on and on and on round the walls of my new life. She even entered my dreams. Sometimes, in these dreams, she was seated on one of those riverboats that I'd seen pictured on the Seine, with Marianne on her knee and a picture-postcard view of Notre Dame cathedral behind her. At other more disconcerting times, she'd got herself to Kensington by some magical means and just walked into the flat near Exhibition Road I now shared with Anthracite and stood looking down at us as we lay in the big bed Felicity had purchased for us from Heal's. It felt to me that she had a look of pity on her face.

This look seemed to be saying, I've got Simon Hurst and you've got Hugo Forster-Pellisier with his pompous name and his lanky orange hair. But life has never been fair. All you can do is go on.

Solange was right about going on. Every morning, Hugo put on his suit and his cycle clips and bicycled from Exhibition Road to New Bond Street. As he left, I put a frail little kiss on his cheek and he patted my stomach, as if to remind me to keep the baby in there and not lose it. Then I'd get dressed in the style of frock people called the Sack Dress to disguise the altered shape of my body, and stare at myself in a long mirror, wondering who I actually was. Because it felt to me that I wasn't now, at the age of twenty, the person I'd imagined I was going to become; I was a kind of hybrid Marianne – half her old passionate teenage self and half somebody else, whom I hadn't got to know yet and who looked downright peculiar. I wanted to understand and appraise this other Marianne, but I couldn't quite get a handle on her.

Sometimes, she felt excited about the baby and surged down on a number 14 bus to Knightsbridge, then walked to Hayford's in Sloane Street to buy dinky little leggings and matinée jackets like the ones we had to knit at Crowbourne House for the orphans of England. At other times, she longed to be far away in some hot place like Sardinia, all alone, drinking Campari under a striped umbrella, while the sea kept on and on breaking and retreating and the evening came on and there was music somewhere and she began walking towards it.

When I thought about Pet, with her furious new

friends and her CND marches and her Study of Every-thing, it seemed to me that she knew exactly why she was alive and where she might be going, and I felt envious of this. I wanted her to come down to London and explain my life to me. I imagined her saying, 'Okey-dokey, girlie, but why not let's mosey over to Wimbledon Common and hire a couple of horses and gallop while we talk?' And as soon as she said this, I said, 'You know, Pet, the only other people I've loved, apart from Simon and you, are horses,' and Pet said, 'Right, except for starters, Marianne, horses aren't people,' and I said, 'Well, they are to me.'

I probably mentioned horses a lot to Anthracite because when the summer started to sidle towards us, he said, 'I want us to have a break from everything before the baby comes. I think we need that and we deserve it. So we'll go to Cornwall. And I don't see why we couldn't do a bit of gentle riding.'

I gave in my notice to Janice Ludlow. She seemed dis-appointed that I couldn't spend the next bit of my life helping her to write the answers to the manifold puzzles of the human condition. I reminded her that I'd never been very good at these answers, but she said, 'I beg to differ, Marianne.' And on my last day behind the Adler, she said, 'I've got a surprise for you. I know you're very attached to that machine, so I've agreed with the editor, you can take it with you and he will ask Personnel to replace it with a newer and lighter model.'

I gave Janice a little kiss. For some reason, I felt that this gift was the most significant thing anybody had ever given me. I wasn't sure why I felt this because I really didn't know what I was going to do with a typewriter and part of me wished it was a sewing machine, but when I knew it was going to be mine, I found myself caressing it gently, just like Simon and I had caressed the bonnet of his pale blue Morris Minor. Then I hauled it out of the building, my legs buckling under the weight of it, and hailed a taxi in Farringdon Street and it rode with me home to Kensington, sitting on the seat beside me, pregnant with all the stories it longed for somebody to write on its keys of iron.

When Hugo came home and saw it sitting on the floor beside our sofa in the flat, he said, 'What's that?' I said, 'Well, Anthracite, check your catalogue, but I think it's a manual writing device, almost certainly German, designed in Frankfurt circa 1957 . . .' and I expected him to laugh, but he only stared at the Adler, as if it were some piece of trash left behind by the dustmen, and said, 'OK, but what are you going to do with it?' And I said, 'I haven't decided. But in the first instance, I'm going to write letters to Pet. When we get back from Cornwall, I'm going to give her news of all the amazing rides we've been on.'

The baby was due in July and now it was May, and on the long drive to Cornwall we saw how the rains of March and April had soaked into the earth of dear old England and nourished all the thousand bright green growing things. We grew silent, looking at these. We'd been in London for so long, we'd somehow forgotten about springtime and acres of young wheat and white lambs, like little clipped and shampooed poodles, jumping about under a blue sky. I didn't know what Hugo was thinking in the quiet of the car, but when I gazed at all this sweetness, my heart did a kind of somersault and I thought, This is what I really love: not London, nor my imaginary Paris, nor even the beaches of Sardinia, but oak trees and hedgerows and narrow English lanes threading along towards hills and tumps.

I turned to Anthracite and said, 'I think we should live in a field, not in Kensington, don't you?' Keeping his eye on the road, Hugo said, 'One day perhaps we will, but not yet.' I said, 'You mean when we're old?' He said, 'Yes,' and I said, 'What's the use of that?' And he said, 'Probably I meant old-ish, when we're still capable of growing runner beans and tomatoes.' So then I got even quieter, suddenly realising for what felt like the first time that not just this bit of my life, but the whole huge and unending thing was going to be lived with Hugo Forster-Pellisier. His orange hair would turn to grey. He would become a director of Sotheby's or of some other auction house. He would begin to look like his father. And I would sit in an old brocaded chair and stare at him and ask myself why this calamity had happened to me and wonder who was responsible for it.

When we got to the rented house, which was the same house we'd been in with our parents on that long-ago holiday, I remembered how large it was and I said to Anthracite, 'I can't quite recall why we need this huge house just for the two of us.'

Standing in the heavily curtained sitting room, Hugo

said, 'The last time we were here, you weren't mine, and now you are. I wanted to revisit everything with my beautiful wife.'

The idea that I somehow 'belonged' to Hugo was a depressing one. I was about to say, 'I don't *belong* to you, Anthracite,' but I stopped myself in time because I was touched by him saying that thing about my beauty. Though my acne had cleared up (Pet had told me that a lot of sex could work miracles on the skin and Hugo never called me a 'lousy fuck'), I knew I wasn't exactly beautiful – my brown hair had a stupid kink in it and my breasts were too small – yet somehow this was the word Hugo had chosen to use. I was reminded what a good sport Anthracite had always been – always on my side when most of the world seemed to be against me – and I kissed his freckled cheek and said, 'When we've unpacked, let's go into the garage and find those old fur coats and put them on and play table tennis, and then after the game we could fuck on the ping-pong table, if you felt that that would move you.'

Hugo said, 'One of the things I love about you, Marianne, is that I absolutely never know what you're going to say next.'

Neither of us knew what was going to *happen* next. We had no idea we were going to become players in a real tragedy.

It unfolded like this. On our second day in Cornwall, Hugo hired us two strong horses and we set out for a gentle trot around the great curve of Constantine Bay. The day was warm but windy, with the white waves sparkling in the sunshine and the sky an innocent blue. To be on a horse again, even at seven months pregnant, with my belly squished in towards the horse's neck, seemed to lift my spirits so wonderfully high that I found myself breaking into a Frank Sinatra song. (I should add here that I've noticed this is what sometimes happens to people when they're visited by a certain lightness of heart: they try to sing a Frank Sinatra song, and I was one of them, even if Pet always found this really embarrassing.) I was singing the bit from 'Nancy (With the Laughing Face)' about my heart being like a charcoal burner when Hugo said, 'Let's canter, shall we?'

We kicked gently and got our horses into the sweet, swaying rhythm of a canter, and I was rocking along, still singing, feeling happier than I'd felt in a long while, when I saw that just ahead of us there were two kids, a girl and a boy, flying a box kite. The kite was riding obediently on the cloudless air and I glimpsed the delight on the faces of the kids and thought, When the baby is born, we must remember to introduce her to the wonders of kite flying. But then, as we drew level with the kids, a sudden gust of wind sent the box kite whirling out on its line and the children were pulled forwards almost into our pathway and my horse reared up in terror and I lost my grip on everything and went hurtling into the sand.

I landed on my back. I could hear the thump my body made as it fell, as if it had been some other bulky thing crashing down beside me. Then I could hear something else, which was the gulping noise I was making, trying to breathe, and I thought, Oh, that's all right then, I'm just winded, and I'll stay here on the wet sand for a while and then I'll try to get to the bit of the song where Frank Sinatra nails the thing about the laughing face, which was my favourite line.

I couldn't quite reach the laughing face, it felt too difficult. Then I saw Hugo's face, not laughing but coming down, as if from on high, and moving just above my face, as if he was trying to talk to me, but I couldn't hear what he was saying. I couldn't hear, I realised, because something else was now going on in my body, something so violent, it commandeered all my senses except one: the feeling of unbearable pain in my head and down all the length of me, especially in the place where the baby was waiting to complete itself. I tried to tell Hugo about this pain, but all I could do was gulp. Hugo put his arms around me and tried to lift me up, but I think I screamed and then what I noticed was that the great immensity of the Cornish afternoon was sort of collapsing in on itself, like things sometimes do at the end of movies, collapse into a tiny white dot, providing you with the understanding that the film is over. And in certain cinemas – in case you erroneously believe that the picture isn't finished when it actually is finished – you get a caption in a circle which says 'That's all Folks'.

I gave birth to a baby girl, but she was dead. I never saw her or held her. She was wrapped in a green cloth and taken away. We'd had a list of names for her – Georgina, Jennifer, Amy, Fiona – but I knew that these names were going to have to disappear too, like the rays of the sun sinking below the horizon, never to come up again.

I lay in my hospital bed in Padstow and bled into the sheets. I was told there was a crack in my pelvis and I imagined this crack as a kind of vast crevasse in the side of an icy mountain, into which my poor dead baby had fallen. I felt such sorrow for her unlived life that I longed to join her. And I thought that perhaps joining her wouldn't be too difficult because I was almost certainly dying. There were voices all round me, urging me to 'hold on', but I couldn't put names to them.

Then I came back from death and recognised my mother. I said, 'Mummy, what are you doing here?' and she started crying and said, 'Oh God, Gerald, she's woken up.' So then Daddy's face swam into view, reddish and scented with du Maurier smoke, and I said, 'Daddy, where have you come from? Shouldn't you be on manoeuvres?' and Daddy said, 'She's talking balderdash, Lal, but at least she's breathing.'

I closed my eyes. I thought floating in my tank of death was more enjoyable than listening to stuff like this. I tried to raise my arm, to gesture to Mummy and Daddy to go away, but my arm was very heavy and it seemed to be attached to something else, as if it belonged to Stewart Granger manacled to the wall in the *Prisoner of Zenda*, so I lowered it again and lay very still. I had the feeling that I was waiting for another face to appear next to mine, but I couldn't remember whose face it was supposed to be.

I floated off into darkness and had an inappropriate dream. I was bleeding all over the back seat of Simon's

Morris Minor, but Simon was lying on top of me, naked from the waist down, with his erect penis coated in my blood, and he was saying, 'It doesn't matter, angel. All that matters is our love for each other. That's the only thing in the world that is precious to me.' Then I felt myself being shaken awake. In my inappropriate dream, I must have called out Simon's name because a stern voice was speaking to me, saying, 'Not Simon, Yeti. Not Simon! It's Hugo.'

Poor Hugo.

He told me once we returned to life in London that he'd had great dreams for his dead daughter. He was going to move us all to Wimbledon so that she could have a pony, housed in some sweet little stable adjacent to the Common. He was going to try to buy a house in Cornwall so that her summer holidays would be filled with the sound of seagulls. He was going to teach her table tennis. He was going to hang a Japanese long sword by Naganobu, c.1858, above the door to her bedroom, to protect her from all harm.

I told him that, as dreams went, these were tender and honourable and I said to him, 'Just save them up, Anthracite, for when we try again for another baby,' but he didn't comment on this; he just he gave me a sorrowing look.

He was becoming a very quiet person. In the mornings, he would leave me sleeping and creep out of the flat, silent as a cat burglar. Sometimes, when he got home, we'd watch *Top of the Pops* together and then he might hum a song for a while but he soon fell back into being this new, silent Hugo, who drank quite a lot of whisky and who sometimes wept when he went to the bathroom.

I felt that I was somehow to blame. If I hadn't fallen off the horse, then we would have had our daughter by now and she would have been baptised in the creamy old christening robes once worn by Felicity Forster-Pellisier, and then later been seated with paternal pride in a high chair, bought from Peter Jones, eating expensive little jars of apricot purée. I kept trying to tell Hugo and tell myself that all might be well in the end, another baby would come along, but Hugo never replied to anything that I uttered along these lines until one evening he said, 'Stop saying that, Marianne. I can't bear for you to say that one more time.'

So then I had to turn to him and say, 'Well, all right, Anthracite. I know there's something you're not telling me. Do you want to say what it is?'

He was drinking his whisky. He kept the bottle near his glass, within reach of his hand. I sat down very close to him and waited for him to speak. He said, 'You're not wrong. I haven't told you. I was just waiting for the right time.'

I didn't like the smell of whisky, but I never told him this because I knew that this kind of remark makes a person seem petulant and self-centred. Hugo topped up his glass and took a slug of the drink that he loved and I hated and then he told me how, after the damage to my pelvis from the fall, followed by the loss of the baby and the bleeding that almost cost me my life, the gynaecologist had taken him into some little space the hospital called a 'family room' to inform him with some solemnity that he would have to give up all hope of having a family. I said, 'That was a piece of irony, Hugo, that he took you into a "family room" to tell you that you could never have a family,' and Hugo said, gently, 'Be quiet, Yeti, and listen.'

He told me that the surgeon went on to say that there was now 'irreparable damage' to my uterus. He didn't say what kind of damage, and that's a thing I don't like about people in the medical profession: they often just give you a few cryptic words and not the whole story. But the surgeon was certain, he said, that any new pregnancy would result in miscarriage and haemorrhage and be very dangerous to my life and that Hugo, as my husband, had to make sure this didn't happen.

I stared at Hugo and what I felt was very complicated. I could understand that for Anthracite this news was a horrible severing of the thread that led from his heart to his hopes for his future, but there was a stubborn bit of me which felt consoled by it. I almost said, 'I longed for my dead daughter, and felt such pity for her, and yet somehow I've never been able to imagine it fully enough, Hugo: a little dynasty of Forster-Pellisiers emerging into the kind of future which sent them to schools like Crowbourne House and gave them Oxford-tainted dreams. I've never been able to believe in it.'

But I didn't say this. An image came to me of Felicity's cream silk christening gown lying in its box, with its shroud of tissue paper – lying there for always and never being taken out to dress a living child – and I made myself think only about this and not remember the pure sorrow of the thing. I got up and went and put my arms around Hugo, trying not to mind the scent of whisky, and I said, 'You know, Anthrax, that doctors can be wrong? They never think they're wrong because they always like to know better than the rest of us. They all imagine they were there in the Garden of Eden, giving instructions to the snake, or something, deciding how everything was going to turn out. But they weren't there. They can only make guesses. It might be that we have loads of children . . .'

'No!' he said. 'We can't. We mustn't. We can't risk it, Marianne. Because when I almost lost you in Padstow, I saw so clearly how much I love you. I've completely loved you ever since that first holiday when you became Yeti. Our wedding day was the happiest moment of my life.'

'Oh,' I said, 'then you've suppressed the moment when I crawled out of the Bentley and was sick in the road?'

Hugo let fall into the silence a tiny shiver of a laugh, then he began crying and I stroked his orange hair. I said, 'We'll go on, Hugo. We'll go on. It's what we're going to do. If we see this as a tragedy, it will never end. We just have to go on and see what happens.'

IV

We went on. We went on like this, in fact, for some years.

We moved to a larger flat in Kensington when Hugo became a director of a small auction house called Riley Mountfitchet with premises on Conduit Street. The flat filled up with nineteenth-century Italian onyx vases and Victorian rosewood bergères. When Pet came to stay with us, she commented that we couldn't move around the flat properly because we had too much furniture. Human existence in our spare room, she announced, was made disagreeable by the 'idiotic' presence of an enormous mahogany armoire. I told her that she could put her clothes in this and that these grateful clothes would feel roomy and comfortable there, but instead of laughing, or even showing the ghost of a smile, she said that she *had* no clothes, only some torn jeans and a leather thong or two. She added in a confiding voice that if you wore tight leather thongs instead of knickers you could sometimes have spontaneous orgasms without touching yourself and I thanked her for this information.

Pet had finished her degree at Essex and was now doing a PhD at the University of Sussex. Her thesis was titled 'Unaltering Patriarchal Attitudes in an Altered World'. She was very serious about her work. She told me that she was looking closely at my life and said, 'If I didn't love you as I do, Marianne, I would say some hurtful things to you.'

I asked her what things and she said, 'The worst thing is that you're becoming like your mother, doing nothing with your time, just existing and being kept by a man.'

'You're right,' I said. 'And I don't love myself one bit. But at least I'm almost succeeding in my escape from the Love Asylum.'

She looked at me with her fierce blue Scottish look and said, 'I see no real sign of that. Try harder.'

I told her that I really had been trying, but then – and I didn't exactly intend to say this to Pet, but I did – as bad luck would have it, I had run into Jasmine in Peter Jones. She was all grown up and suddenly beautiful and studying to be a vet. Jasmine and I had stood side by side in the fabric department, fingering velveteen, and she told me that Simon was still attempting to become a writer.

Pet cut me off here and said in her snarky voice, 'Attempting? Writers either *are writers*, or they're not. So what's the paragon trying to write *about*?' and I said I didn't know because I hadn't been interested enough to ask. Pet scowled at me and said, 'One of the things the Women's Movement is teaching me, Marianne, is to be truthful and to tell things like they are. Women will never gain their proper place in society if they take refuge in untruth.'

So then I felt even more ashamed of myself. I knew

that I still thought about Simon far too much. I told myself that this was better than thinking about my dead daughter. I pictured him walking down a Paris street and going into a café and ordering an espresso in a tiny little white china cup. I could see the cup very clearly and then his mouth as he began to drink a minuscule amount of strong black coffee. I thought about him walking home from the café and going to the heavy door of some apartment block and going up to the second floor in an antique old elevator and getting out and walking along a corridor to his flat, hearing the sounds of little Marianne's voice as he got his key out of his pocket, but hoping she wouldn't disturb him as he tried to get back to the novel or story he was writing. I said to Pet, 'I suppose I can't really pretend, not to you. He's just there in my heart, Pet, and I fear that he always will be.'

Pet said, 'So where's Hugo in all this?' and I said, 'Hugo loves me, and that's all there is to say.'

Pet looked exasperated. She was regal these days, like a male rock star. She'd cut her crazy hair very short and wore mutilated men's clothes over her leather underwear. I thought, If Pet gets so infuriated with me that she breaks off our friendship, I will feel more alone than I can bear. I went to her and she put her arms around me and I said, 'I know I've disappointed you for a long time, Ms Macintyre, but I don't know how to be any different.'

She kissed the top of my head. We were standing in my kitchen, near a ceramic butler sink Hugo had bought from a country house sale, and I thought how I had always liked the smell of her, which was the smell of our

123

shared past. I lifted my head and looked up at her and she smiled. I think she knew that I was wondering, right there in the kitchen, what it would be like to go to bed together, because she broke away from me and said, 'Put something significant in your life, Marianne. Not me. I'm not the answer. You have to search and find.'

I imagined myself applying for a lowly job with a riding stables. In spite of my accident, my feelings about the nobility of horses hadn't changed. I wondered if the Household Cavalry took on broken-hearted, childless women to groom their black and shining mounts. Hugo was sympathetic to my wonderings. I knew that anything I wanted, Hugo would try to get for me, that's the ridiculous power of love, but I also knew that nothing was going to come of this idea.

Then I did something which surprised me. I got the old Adler out of the bottom of the George III wardrobe to which it had been consigned and set it up on a small table in my bedroom. I dusted off all the years of neglect and bought a new ribbon for it and some blindingly white paper and a packet of carbons, dark and blue as the Saltire. What I wanted to write was a story about a horse. I decided the horse was a stallion who came from Argentina and whose name was Diego, which was the only Argentinian name I knew. I said to Pet, 'I think you're going to be OK with this, because all stories about horses are about love and freedom,' and she said, 'All right, but just try to avoid it being sentimental.'

I wanted to tell the story from Diego's point of view. I

thought some of my readers might complain that horses can't think in actual words, so can't be the narrators of stories, but I imagined telling them that one of the things I didn't like in some of the novels I read was when everybody who's speaking sounds exactly the same, so you don't know who's feeling what. I would say that in my little book, you would know all the time that you were in Diego's consciousness because of how he spoke and thought, in a way that was unique to him, so you would never feel confused and think it was a human person speaking; all you would care about would be Diego's horse destiny.

When I told Anthracite that I was going to write a story about an Argentinian stallion, I thought he might laugh at me, but one of the many nice things about Hugo is that he never laughs at me. He just said, 'That's great, Yeti,' like I'd told him I'd got tickets for the Chelsea Flower Show. Then he moved right away from this subject and said, 'By the way, we're going to Paris for a few days in September.'

Paris.

I thought at once, I don't think I can do that: be in the same city as Simon. I sort of knew that wherever I walked, along every boulevard and narrow street, I'd be looking at every passer-by, wondering if out of the throng his beautiful face was going to appear and if it did, whether I was going to fall down in the street.

I asked Hugo why we were going to Paris and he told me that he'd been told about a tiny shop which sold nothing but eighteenth- and nineteenth-century puppet theatres and that Riley Mountfitchet wanted to 'test the waters' for these wonders in London. He said, 'In the antiques market, we should keep much more of an eye on Paris. There are *niche* objects there which you can no longer find here. Rents are lower, so more off-the-wall premises can keep going. London is pricing itself out of everything but fashion and food.'

I was about to suggest to Hugo that he go to Paris without me because I would be working on my story about Diego, but considering that I hadn't even started on it, only stared at the wedge of white paper and the soft blue skin of the carbons, wondering if I really knew what the word *pampas* actually denoted, this felt very lame. Instead, I said, 'If we're going to Paris, Hugo, can I go to Harvey Nichols and buy a couple of new outfits?' And he said, 'Of course you can. And we'll stay at the Crillon Hotel.' Money in our household had never seemed to be a problem. When Daddy had sent me ten pounds for my birthday, Hugo had said, 'I actually think that's bloody stingy,' which it was, but I also knew that it irked Daddy to realise that the Forster-Pellisiers were much richer than he had ever been or ever would be.

Paris.

I couldn't stop thinking about it. I wondered whether to contact Jasmine, to find out which street Simon and Solange lived in. I'd imagined this street a thousand times, but it was a street of the mind, not an actual place. I bought a map of Paris, which was sold as a tiny little confusing book, with separate pages for each arrondissement and it was hard to learn anything from it unless you already knew it, and I thought trying to learn French with Mam'zelle Charrier had been like this: you knew all the information was right there in her head, but getting it out of her head and into yours was unbearably difficult.

Eventually, I found the rue de Grenelle, which was in the 7th Arrondissement. This was the street where Simon had first lodged with Madame Louvel and where he'd slept with Solange and changed his life and mine forever, but I somehow knew that he wouldn't be there any more, living with his mother-in-law and his daughter called Marianne. It looked like a very long street and already I imagined myself trudging along it, step by slow step, looking up at all the windows, wondering if Simon's face was suddenly going to appear at one of them, and then, when it didn't, returning to the hotel and Hugo and a conversation about puppet theatres, which I knew would be of no real interest to me.

Meanwhile, I began my story narrated by Diego, the Argentinian stallion. I gave him quite good descriptive powers. I wanted to make him the Charles Dickens of the equine world, describing places with great zest, but leaving out all the hilarious made-up names because I didn't think names would be his strong point. Diego roamed about on the pampas, telling us about the scent of the grass at twilight and the blue forest of the night skies. He described drinking from icy streamlets which bubbled up from the gentle hills. Sometimes, he told us, he whinnied at the full moon.

I showed this opening bit to Pet when she came to

visit the next time and she sat in a Louis XV beechwood fauteuil turning over the pages impatiently, as if she thought she was imminently about to get to something really good and then discovered that this something really good wasn't actually there. When she'd finished all the pages, she looked up at me and said, 'Nothing much happens in this story, Marianne. You just go on about the landscape.'

I said, 'Yes, but Dickens goes in for a lot of description, and something is *going* to happen, Pet. The main thing that is going to happen is that Diego is going to meet the boy.'

'What boy?'

'I don't have a name for him, because Diego isn't good at names. He's just "the boy". He's going to care for Diego and, like him, the boy loves the pampas grass and the big skies and the streams and everything, so I have to go on about these at the beginning, I have to *establish* all this, because I hate it in a story when you're told to care about a character losing something, but you've never experienced the thing they've actually lost. If you don't describe the lost thing to the readers, it's impossible for them to care about it one way or another.'

'OK,' said Pet. 'Aye. I think you're right about that. But there's still too much about starlight and grass. Don't have all this at the beginning. It puts readers off. What they want is jeopardy.'

I was just beginning to try out a new opening to my story when we left for Paris. We flew from Heathrow Airport

128

and there was something about the scent of jet fuel which made me feel both excited and afraid, as though I was about to try to conquer the universe, wearing only a purple dress from Biba.

A taxi took us from the airport to the Hôtel de Crillon on the Place de la Concorde. This felt like entering a pretend world, a beautifully constructed film set, where thin young boys in burgundy uniforms danced a ballet with shining luggage trolleys, and where the ghosts of a thousand floor polishers whispered in the scented air.

As we waited to check in, Hugo said, 'Swivel your eyes left, Yeti, and you'll see Tony Curtis.' So I looked over to a light-filled cabinet displaying jewels and perfumes and standing right before it was the star of *Some Like It Hot* in all his impossible sweetness. I thought, Well, perhaps we *are* in a film set after all. I gazed at Tony Curtis for so long that my eyes began to feel dry, but these dry eyes also noted that he was wearing built-up shoes, and I had the thought that if you can become an object of universal longing and still feel twitchy about your height, what hope is there for happiness upon this earth? So I looked back towards the bellboys in their boxy hats and when I next turned my head in the direction of Tony Curtis, he had gone. I said to Hugo, 'All the good things vanish away. They say, "That's all Folks!" and then they're gone,' but Hugo wasn't listening.

Our bedroom at the Crillon looked out over the *place*. I stood at our window, watching the Citroëns and the mopeds whizzing round it in a kind of jocular cavalcade. I thought, Everything in Paris looks as if it's practising the waltz, whereas quite a lot of things in London – like the choked-up buses in Piccadilly I saw on the first night of my honeymoon – appear as if they've just come out of hospital after a leg operation and are learning to walk from scratch. And then I thought this was perhaps what Simon fell in love with, this *dance* of all the thousand moving things in Paris, so then he wanted to join in and Solange was his ticket to belonging here and learning all the intricate steps of the city. And then he never left.

While I was having this reverie, I suddenly heard Hugo say, 'You'd better change for dinner, Marianne.' I thought how like Daddy he suddenly sounded and what came over me was another wave of weariness with my life with Anthracite. I lived among beautiful furniture, but it was very old furniture and the flat was dark, as if it should have been the home of an elderly person with light-sensitive eyes. Nothing wonderful or surprising ever seemed to happen there. Pet dared to say to me that the place was suffocating me. And the years were passing . . .

I turned and looked at my husband, who was buttoning up a pale blue shirt with a stiff white collar. I had a wicked yearning to be alone in this expensive hotel room, to lie in the big brocaded bed, wearing a leather thong, and dream of Simon and then get up at dawn, as the sun was beginning to glitter on the cobblestones of the *place*, and get out my map of Paris and find my way to the rue de Grenelle and then walk slowly along it, shouting Simon's name. 'O Captain! My Captain, come to me! Come to me!' I would have called and he would have appeared at last, standing by a heavy door, and when he saw me, he would have broken down in tears, like he once did in Cordelia Pratt's single bed, with the voice of Ella Fitzgerald just audible downstairs: *'If they asked me, I could write a book . . .'*

The next day, I went with Hugo to the tiny shop which sold puppet theatres. It was in a street called the rue des Saints-Pères, which I thought translated as the Street of the Holy Fathers, and I said to Hugo that in my view this sounded a bit Irish, but he didn't laugh. He just snapped at me and said, 'It's not Irish, Marianne. Why don't you try to learn things as they actually are?' He strode on ahead of me, up the tilting street, and I knew that he was hurt because of what had happened the night before. We'd had a sumptuous dinner in the restaurant at the Crillon, which included a dish of minuscule eels – *anguillettes* – shining like silverfish, and I'd got drunk on Chablis and when he wanted to make love to me in the big bed, I just pushed him away and fell into a fretful sleep and then woke up again and was sick in the gilded bathroom, and when I got back into the bed, he told me he still loved me but that I was becoming 'a bloody difficult person to like'.

I thought for a long time about this, but I didn't know what to do with the information. In my life with Hugo, I felt, all the time, that I was doing the best I could, but now I knew for sure that my 'best' resembled the antics of a stricken kind of creature, like a sick grey parrot in a cage.

The puppet theatres sold in the Street of the Holy

Fathers were things of intricate beauty. Hugo's auction-eer's soul was so moved by them, his body began to give off a sudden radiant heat. The two shop assistants, who were old and pale, as though they'd never left the little shop in many years, could scent this heat and looked alarmed. If I'd been able to speak proper French, I would have told them that they didn't have to worry: what Hugo was radiating was excitement and he would pay a good price for these tiny little stages with their dancing men and women and their trees of painted wire.

I think the old men eventually understood this because they showed us how to move the puppets around, hold-ing little crosses made of bone. One of these was a puppet in the form of little girl wearing a calico smock and her cross was put into my hands and the two old gentlemen nodded at me encouragingly, as if to say, 'There you are, you're a young woman who must surely be a mother, so you will know how to move the child.' For a little while, I made the girl dance, then I laid her down. I laid her down as if she were dead. I felt so sad, I had to move away from the tiny stage and walk out of the shop and I turned left and ran towards the river.

I stood looking down at the water. The sky was white and luminous and the river was the colour of milky tea. I watched a bateau-mouche tourist boat, which just looked like a floating dining room, come gliding by and I thought how, if I had had Hugo's child, my Georgina or my Amy, we could have taken her on one of these and she would have eaten moules marinière and chips and watched Paris go sailing past her, like things you don't completely understand go sailing past you in dreams. She would have been about ten by now and might be sensitive about her red hair.

I expected that Hugo would come and find me once he'd agreed a price for the puppet theatre, but I stood staring at the river for a long time and he didn't appear and I thought again about the thing he'd said about my being 'difficult to like' and knew that it was true. I went about life like the tooth fairy, pretending that I existed, but in fact getting everyone else to snatch away all the fallen and discarded things in human lives and replace them with silver, because I had no silver to give.

I turned away from the water. I stood on the pavement, waiting for a Citroën taxi to come by, and when one stopped and swooped me up, I told the driver to go to the rue de Grenelle. From my mispronunciation of the word Grenelle, he worked out that I was from England and he kept turning round and saying, 'Swinging London, *n'est-ce pas*?' to me and I wanted to say, 'I'd prefer it if you drove with your eyes looking at the road ahead,' but instead I said, 'Well, it *was* swinging, but now that's pretty much over and we've got strikes and power cuts and miners on the dole and when I watch the news on TV I have to close my eyes.'

When we got to the rue de Grenelle, the cabbie asked me which part of it I wanted. We were near a small restaurant called La Petite Chaise, which had a few wooden tables on the pavement and a sparse little hedge growing round them in zinc tubs, and I thought I would like to go and sit down there and quench a raging thirst with a

Coca-Cola and wait for Simon to appear. So I got out and paid the driver and while he fussed over the change he said, 'You a swinging lady?' and I said, 'Absolutely not, I'm just in the process of turning into my mother.' He looked baffled and drove away with the kind of angry leap that Citroëns seem able to make better than other kinds of car and I had the random thought that I might ask Hugo if I could exchange my Renault 4, which Pet said resembled a surgical boot, for a Citroën Dyane, which was much more like a wallaby. I thought that being able to leap around in a car might cheer me up and make me nicer to live with, but I was far from certain that it would. I wondered if I was destined to be nasty forever now.

I sat down by the hedge of La Petite Chaise. No waiter came out, so I just lurked there like a dumb tourist, gazing up and down the street. Opposite was a little apartment block, not very tall, and from an upstairs window I could hear someone practising piano scales. I wondered if this could be Simon's daughter, the other Marianne, a teenager now. I could imagine her hair, which would be brown and soft like Simon's, falling towards the keyboard and her delicate fingers caressing the notes with infinite care.

One or two people came past. I was tempted to ask a mature man who lingered near the hedge for a moment, brushing a piece of lint from the shoulder of his overcoat, if he knew the Louvel family. I practised how to say this in my mind: *S'il vous plait, Monsieur, connaissez-vous la famille Louvel?* But by the time I'd got the words in the right order, the man had got rid of the lint and moved away, leaving behind the slightly invasive scent of patchouli. The piano scales went on. Still no waiter came, so then I realised that La Petite Chaise was actually closed, despite the tables on the pavement, so I got up and began to walk left down the rue, with my heart doing a double kind of beating; it was beating in the expectation that Simon was just about to appear and it was beating with the sorrow that he wouldn't.

I walked on. The sound of the piano scales followed me for a while and then faded. The sun came out. I noticed that some of the men I passed caressed me with their eyes and it suddenly occurred to me that with my acne long gone, it was possible that I had become very slightly beautiful. So then I thought, If this turns out to be the case, then everything will probably be all right. I will ask Hugo to forgive me. I will try to become easier to like. I will buy an icy Coca-Cola to quench my never-ending thirst.

V

Soon after our return from Paris, I got a call from Daddy.

'Trouble at mill,' he said. 'Mummy's in hospital with pneumonia. Better get down here, Mops.'

Daddy only called me 'Mops' when he had a rare moment of pure love for me or when he wanted something from me, or on the very infrequent occasions when he felt afraid. I said, 'Right, Daddy. Are you telling me Mummy's going to die?'

'You know your mother,' he said. 'Stubborn as a tail gunner. But she's bloody poorly. Went out to play bridge with Angela Fletcher-Blake and caught a chill from an open window and bang, pulmonary collapse: surrender at Arnhem! Will that little cereal packet of a car you drive make it down the M4?'

'Yes,' I said. 'Of course it will. Shall I bring groceries or are you coping OK?'

'Living on pheasant,' said Daddy. 'Found ten of them in the deep freeze. Just thaw them out and bung them in the Aga. Stone Age diet, what?'

I said I would buy some vegetables to go with the pheasant and a few other necessities, like chocolate digestive biscuits and grapes for Mummy. By the time Hugo got home from work, I had the Renault 4 refuelled and packed, with the Adler typewriter sitting on the front seat, ready to play the part of the supportive companion. All Hugo said was, 'Well gosh, poor Lal.' So I kissed his freckled nose and departed into the London rush hour, with a Nina Simone tape playing in my car.

I suppose it was mean of me, but I felt light-hearted as I reached the motorway. Perhaps it was the effect of Nina Simone's wonderfully angry voice, but although in one corner of my mind was sympathy for Mummy, squashing that sympathy into an almost invisible mass was a kind of hectic excitement that something completely unexpected had happened. In my life with Hugo, the component parts were endlessly and endlessly identical, even as day followed day. I made breakfast for him, usually eggs and bacon, and saw him off to work in his suit and his bicycle clips. Then I looked at *The Times* for about ten minutes, or for as long as I could bear to read about strikes and wounded miners and the general darkness of England's soul. Then I did nothing for a long time. Then I lay in the bath, topping it up with more and more hot water, to prolong its soothing state. Sometimes, I put on a Charles Aznavour record and swooned along to that for a while. Then I ate a Marmite sandwich and sat at my work table in front of the Adler and worked on my story about Diego. I'd got the boy into the story and described the little house made of cob where the boy lived with his grandmother and I'd set up the makeshift stable he and his friends had constructed to shelter Diego from the cold nights of winter. I quite liked all this, but I couldn't work for very long each day. I thought about old Hemingway sitting for hours in the Café de Flore, eking out small cups of coffee, writing on and on and never tiring of his own thoughts, and I wished that I never tired of mine, but I always did.

Sometimes, on fine days, I went out and walked about in Kensington, or went to the park or met somebody or other for tea in the Roof Gardens of Derry & Toms. Hugo and I had made a few friends, but not many, and none I really cared about. I missed Pet. Often, I came back to the flat and wrote her a letter on the Adler telling her about my empty life. Sometimes – most days – I just came back and did nothing again, listened to a Bob Dylan song or else cleaned a bit of silver or tidied a drawer, or prepared a meal for Hugo and me – things like lamb chops with mashed potato and chicken stew with butter beans – to eat in near silence. When he got back from Riley Mountfitchet, we drank. I drank gin and he drank whisky. We passed an hour this way. Our heads began to spin with terror at life's passing, so we drank some more. Then we ate my meal and watched the TV news and did the dishes and then went to bed, saying, 'Night-night, Hugo,' 'Night-night, Marianne,' very affectionately and then turning away from each other and trying to reach oblivion as quickly as possible.

But now, on the M4, Nina Simone and I were speeding towards Hastings House and Daddy with his frozen pheasants and Mummy trying to breathe, wearing a floral hospital gown, tied at the back. This sudden alteration to everything felt strangely like an unexpected gift.

*

When I got to the house, Daddy wasn't there. A scribbled notice sellotaped to the door knocker read: *Gone to see Mummy. Key in left hand bay tree flower pot.* And I thought it was bad luck on the neighbourhood burglars that they hadn't tried to burgle Hastings House at this precise moment, when they could have just snatched up the front door key from the shrub tub and walked in and begun bagging up Mummy's collection of Delft china and her ivory brush-and-comb set, not to mention Granny Violet's emerald choker, and drunk all the sherry and whisky on the sideboard.

I unpacked the Renault, took the Adler up to my room and stood staring at everything. It was a long time since I'd been in the room. When Hugo and I visited Mummy and Daddy, it was usually only for lunch. Mummy had sort of made it clear to me that having us to stay made demands on her which she didn't want to meet. She'd said to Anthracite, 'Old age comes more quickly to our generation, Hugo, because of what we went through in the war, and you and Marianne will just have to accept what we can and can't do.'

I was tempted to lie down on my old single bed and float into a Simon reverie, but since my visit to the rue de Grenelle, I'd promised myself that I would try not to indulge in any more of these. Being in Paris – walking its streets, smelling its river, seeing how the city arranged itself differently from London – had convinced me that Simon would be there forever, becoming a kind of naturalised French person, and that if we ever met again, there might be a language problem between us.

I walked around the house. Lying about everywhere were old copies of the *Telegraph* and full ashtrays and dirty whisky and sherry glasses and used handkerchiefs and empty du Maurier packets. Clearly, army discipline hadn't taught Colonel Clifford how to run a solitary day-to-day life without leaving behind him multiple sowings of human garbage. I began collecting up the glasses and the handkerchiefs and parking them in the kitchen, which itself was the kind of nauseating sight that I can't bear to describe. There used to be a very nice lady from Weston Applegate village called Mrs Revens who came to clean the house twice a week, but it looked as though she hadn't been there for a long time and when I looked out of the kitchen window, I saw that the lawn was like a hayfield and the flower beds were full of weeds, so I understood that, over and beyond Mummy's pneumonia, there was a calamity going on at Hastings House.

I looked up the number for Mrs Revens in Mummy's phone book and rang it. When Mrs Revens answered, I asked her how long it had been since she'd come to help out in the house and I heard her sigh. 'Oh, crikey,' she said. 'I haven't been there for more than two months now. I would have stayed on, Marianne, but your father took me aside and told me they just couldn't afford to pay me any more. Colonel and Mrs Clifford always treated me kindly, but I can't work for nothing, it's not moral.'

'No,' I said. 'Of course you can't work for nothing. But now I was wondering . . .' I told her about Mummy being in the hospital and the mess the house was in after Daddy had been alone in it for only a few days. I asked her if I could pay her to come and give me a hand to straighten things up a bit and she sighed again and said, 'I'd do it, dear, for all your sakes, but I've got other work now and I do get tired in the afternoons . . .' I told her that I understood and asked after Mr Revens, who had worked on the railways and had now retired with his wife to a council house in Weston Applegate to grow dahlias. Mrs Revens said it had been a good year for these flowers and that Mr Revens had been out every morning, searching for slugs at dawn, 'and so the dahlias had come on really nice'. I said I was pleased about this and then I wished her well and hung up. As I put the phone down, I thought, So that's how it's turned out for Mummy and Daddy: they're alone now because the money's almost gone. They never thought this would happen to them, but it has. Trouble has washed up here in a sickly tide.

By the time Daddy got back from the hospital, I'd got rid of all the empty du Maurier packets and washed the glasses and cleared the rotting food from the kitchen, opened all the windows to let in the autumn breeze and prepared an omelette and salad for supper. Daddy gave me one of his hugs, which had hardly ever been proper hugs, but only a sort of clutching of his hands on my arms to bring me to within touching distance of his shoulder. He looked undone. His eyes appeared milky and startled, his skin was blotchy and pale and there was a sudden sprouting of hair from parts of him where I'd never seen any hair before, like his nostrils and his ears.

He sank down in his favourite armchair in the sitting

room and I sat opposite him and said, 'So tell me how Mummy is.'

He looked all around him, his eyes darting to this thing and that, as if searching for a precious object he'd mislaid, then he said, 'Hospitals are an absolute farce.'

'What d'you mean, Daddy?' I said.

'Tubes,' he said. 'Far too many. Up her nose. Down her throat. Things dribbling into her veins everywhere. Lal could barely move or speak. I wanted to say to the nurses, take all this stuff away, so that I can have a proper conversation with my wife. I wanted to say, look, I was wounded in Germany in '45. I've seen my share of dying. But we never used to go in for all this tube racket.'

I wasn't sure what to say to this, beyond offering to pour Daddy a Scotch and water, which he refused to let me make. He said I'd 'get it all wrong'. Ever since my bad school reports, Daddy seemed to have formed the opinion that his only child suffered from perpetual uselessness. I wanted to remind him that I used to be very good at riding and that I'd married a kind man who could, at a glance, date and value nineteenth-century Italian overmantel mirrors and Directoire-style brass-mounted bonheurs du jour, but I just kept silent and watched Daddy lurch over to the sideboard where he kept his whisky and look all around him for ice, as though he expected to find this in some inappropriate place, such as in the log basket or on top of a pile of Mummy's *Vogue*s. I got up and said I would get some ice from the kitchen. Daddy didn't thank me, he just began rattling an almost empty soda siphon, to encourage the last little jet out of it, then went to the window and stared at the unmown lawn.

I returned without the ice. I told Daddy the ice compartment of the fridge was so clogged up it was frozen shut, and he said, 'Never mind. Who needs it? Ice is an American craze, anyway. They even drink their tea with ice. Where's the comfort in that?'

We didn't talk much about Mummy. I kept asking questions: how, exactly, had Mummy got so ill so suddenly? Was there any idea about when she might recover? And Daddy kept saying he was 'in the bloody dark', that he didn't know a 'bloody thing', that Lal had just been whisked away in an ambulance, 'from one bloody minute to the next', that hospitals were 'worse than prisons' and that he was 'bloody exhausted'. I told him that he could rest the following day; I would visit Mummy and try to talk to a doctor about what was happening to her. He nodded his agreement to this, then asked me if my 'tin can of a car' was up to driving to Reading.

'I don't know,' I said. 'It brought me here from London, but I'll go and ask it.'

I went out into the garden and stood near the shivering birch tree, taking deep breaths of the clear Berkshire air. Then I walked to my car and gave it an affectionate little pat. The Renault 4 and I noticed that the sun was beginning to go down and we could hear rooks squabbling in the far beech tops.

When I got to the hospital ward, I could see what Daddy had meant about this being a bit like a prison. Mummy's bed was crammed into a tiny little space just a few feet from the adjacent patient, who was being sick into an enamel bowl. The bed had its metal side bars raised, designed to keep Mummy from falling onto the linoleum floor, and, just as Daddy had described, a mangrove forest of tubing, leading from parts of her body to bleeping monitors, kept her pinioned in one prone position.

There were no chairs for visitors to sit on, so I sort of clawed my backside onto the tiny bit of the end of the bed not occupied by Mummy's legs and perched there and waited for her to open her eyes. I studied her sleeping face. Her skin was blue-pale. And for some reason, I remembered how she'd looked on that first visit to Cornwall, when she and Felicity Forster-Pellisier had lugged a picnic to the beach and laughed as they handed out the food and how both women had seemed happy and quaintly beautiful in the Cornish sunshine.

Mummy's limp arm (the one not pierced by any cannulas) lay outside the thin hospital blanket. Gently, I picked up her hand and held it in mine.

I said, 'It's Marianne, Mummy. I wonder if you'd like to be awake for a bit?'

I waited and watched to see if she would stir, but she didn't. I wondered if she was really awake but didn't want to try to talk to me and so pretended that she was unconscious. I think a lot of patients in crowded hospitals decide that sleep is just about the best condition they can hope for, and looking all around me, I couldn't really blame them. Mostly one thinks of British Suffering as an almost silent and withheld kind of brand, but here in this ward there was very noisy, high-fidelity, un-British suffering going on, much more You Kay style, with people crying and coughing and swearing and bringing up their food and pressing their buzzers for nurses. I decided Daddy had been right when he'd mentioned the word 'farce'. I didn't see how anyone could recover from anything in these kinds of conditions.

After a while, I laid down Mummy's cold hand and went to find a doctor. I was told there was one 'on his rounds', so I stood by the nurses' station to wait for him and listened to the nurses and the ward sister having a conversation about Paul Newman, whom they all judged to be the most beautiful man on the earth. One of the nurses said, 'If you were married to Paul Newman, you wouldn't have to worry about anything ever again, would you?' I wanted to say, 'Well, I think you might have to worry about quite a lot of things, in particular that he would tire of you and go off with a French girl from the rue de Grenelle.' They all turned to look at me, and so I wondered if I'd actually said all this stuff aloud, without really intending to, but then I realised they weren't looking at me, but at the doctor, who was standing right behind me.

Doctors behave like gods in hospitals. Pet had told me this. 'Not God,' she'd suggested, 'but Greek gods, who do the most capricious things like turning women into bits of forestry and disguising themselves as rapacious swans.' So I turned round to contemplate this particular god and saw that he wasn't Greek at all, but Indian. He had the kind of lean, clever face I'd always imagined for Amar Nath Chatterjee. I said, 'I know you must be very busy,

Doctor, but I would like to talk to you about Mrs Lavender Clifford, in Ward F.'

'Are you a family member?' he asked.

I told him I was Mrs Clifford's only child. (I knew that most people in India belong to large families and so they might possibly feel pity for lonely women who've never known the protection of macho brothers.) I said, 'If you could maybe give me some idea of what we can expect . . .'

'Well,' he said briskly, and without a seeming shred of pity for my only-child status, 'she has pneumonia. Rest, oxygen, antibiotics . . . that's all we can do for her. If her ability to breathe deteriorates further, she may need to go into Intensive Care. We shall see. Meanwhile, she must be kept comfortable and quiet. All right?'

'It's not quiet in the ward,' I said.

The Indian god turned to the nurses. 'Is there some disturbance in F Ward? Disruptive factors?'

'No, certainly not, Doctor,' said the nurse who'd wanted to be married to Paul Newman, so the god turned back to me and said, 'There is just a normal amount of noise in your mother's ward. You are perhaps unfamiliar with hospital conditions?'

'Well,' I said, 'I'm familiar with them now. And I can't see how my mother can recover properly with people vomiting and crying all around her. She needs peace and quiet.'

The god sighed. Pet had told me that in the Greek myths, the male gods always had well-constructed, nimble plans for their crazy exploits and just barged on with them, so I'd never imagined them sighing or looking as though they didn't know what to say next.

'I'm sorry,' said the doctor, 'but I have to finish my rounds. I'm already running late. If you wish to pay for a private room, you must see the ward secretary. Does your family have health insurance?'

I wanted to say that I was pretty sure this was the kind of thing that Daddy had long ago taken care of, but then I remembered the state of entropy at Hastings House and the overgrown garden and the sacking of Mrs Revens and so I said I didn't know whether we did or whether it had been cancelled.

'Well,' said the god, 'please let us know, Miss Clifford. And now . . .'

'Won't you just come and have a look at my mother?'

'No. There is no need. I saw your mother this morning at eight thirty. She is doing as well as can be expected. Please stop your worrying.'

'Why's she so pale and cold?'

'She has been medicated to bring down her fever. She will almost certainly be fine.'

The god marched off, his white coat flying, his shiny black shoes pounding the lino and the ward sister scurrying like a courtier to catch him up. The nurses stared after him in awe. I found I was still holding the packet of digestive biscuits I'd brought for Mummy, so I opened this and offered the biscuits round and all the nurses took one and I took one, too, and we stayed silent for a moment, crunching and munching while all the commotion of life in the ward went on a few feet from where we stood.

*

When I got back to Mummy's bed, she was awake. I kissed her cold forehead. She had difficulty talking, but I understood her to say that she wanted me to read to her.

'Read what, Mummy?' I asked.

She didn't seem to know how to answer this. She just gaped helplessly at me. All she'd read in her lifetime – or this is how it had appeared to me – were magazines, so I looked around the ward to see if I could locate any of these among the medicines and water beakers and half-finished bits of knitting on the locker tops, but I couldn't see one. I was about to get up and go and ask the nurses if any of them had a copy of *Vogue* when I remembered that in my bag, next to the digestives and a bag of grapes, were a few crumpled carbons from my half-finished story. I'd taken to carrying these pages round wherever I went, in a downright pitiful way, so that they wouldn't be lost. They had come to feel like things of value to me and seeing them there gave me a sudden idea. I took them out and said to Mummy, 'All I've got is something I wrote. Do you want me to read that?'

She looked totally confused, as though I'd uttered a sentence in Spanish. I held out the carbons and said, 'This is the work I'm doing now. It's probably no good at all, but it soothes my mind somehow. Shall I just read a bit of that?'

'A bit of what?'

'Of my story. The one I'm writing. It's set on the Argentinian pampas. The character who's narrating it is a horse.'

Mummy's face creased into a grimace. 'What rot!' she said. 'I never heard such rot.'

'You're right,' I said. 'Probably a load of bunkum. And I'm not exactly Hemingway. But I'll read a bit, shall I, and when you want me to stop, just say "Stop!" or put your hand up?'

'Why a horse?' asked Mummy.

'I don't know,' I said. 'It just *is*.'

Because the ward was so cramped, the occupants of the beds on either side of Mummy's had been able to hear every word of this little exchange. The woman on the right had stopped vomiting and was staring at me over a handkerchief pressed to her mouth. The woman on the left, who had been playing patience on a metal meal tray, paused in her game and looked at me expectantly. So I thought that even if Mummy didn't really want to hear my story, perhaps these strangers did, so I sat down and edged my bottom onto the far corner of Mummy's bed and began:

'It was in the winter of that year that the boy found me and gave me my name. He gave me the name Diego. He used to ride me bareback over the pampas and he cared for me and called me his "beautiful one", his beautiful horse, Diego.

'The boy built a shelter for me. It was made of wood and mud, with a little roof of dry reeds. When the nights were cold, I was tethered in there and a worn rug was put over my back and I lay down on dry straw and I thought how lucky I was, now, to be cared for by the boy.

'Then, one morning, which was a bright and fair morning, with lines of sunlight glimmering through the reeds, I waited for the boy to come and untie my tether and bring me water and a pan of oats, but he didn't come. I waited all day. I was very

hungry and thirsty. The night came back and still there was no sign of the boy, so I lay down and tried to sleep. I thought, He will come tomorrow. But the next dawn came and I was still tied up and alone . . .'

I paused in the reading and looked up. Mummy was staring at me. 'Go on,' she said.

At the weekend, Hugo drove down to Hastings House. He seemed very pleased to see me – as if we'd been separated for a long time – and when Daddy went off to the hospital, he took me upstairs and made love to me in a harsh, passionate kind of way, as he hadn't done for several months.

Afterwards, I lay in my narrow bed, hurting, while Hugo went outside and got the rotary lawn mower started. I listened to him going back and forth, pushing the heavy machine into the tangle of grass and flowers. One of the things that I'd always quite liked about Hugo was his energetic aversion to things when they seem *wrong*. He has to try to put them right: a hoover which doesn't vacuum properly; a fire which doesn't draw; a lawn which has become a field. And then I thought, not for the first time, that he'd always known there was something wrong with *me*, a failure to love him as he wanted to be loved, and he spent a good part of his life trying to put this right – but it still wasn't right. And then I wondered whether he knew this or not. I heard Pet's voice say, 'What? Of course he knows. Don't lay any flattering unction to your fickle soul, Marianne. He gets through life by loving for both of you. Otherwise, it would all collapse.' And I knew deep in my heart that what she said was true.

When Daddy got home, he was so pleased to see the lawn looking more like a lawn that he opened a bottle of red wine to drink with the fillet steaks Hugo had brought down from Harrods Food Hall. I cooked them for the shortest time on the hottest of the Aga plates and made a salad and fried potatoes to go with them, and Daddy said this was the best meal he'd eaten in a long time. He looked, suddenly, like happy old kings look in fairy stories, all ruddy and puffed up, with their white hair standing on end in a crownish kind of way. He got up and took a second bottle of wine out of the sideboard cupboard and yanked it open and sloshed it into our glasses and then said, 'Now to other business. Anybody want to hear the latest local shocker?'

'Let me guess,' I said. 'Nobody wants to work for you any more.'

'Damn right. They don't. They want wages I can't afford on an army pension. But that's not it. No, no. It's the Hurst family. Got the boy Simon back living with them. Imagine that. He must be thirty, if he's a day. Lost his pitiful job and his French wife kicked him out, so now he's having some kind of breakdown. That's what I heard in Newbury.'

'Heard from whom?' I said.

'Angela Fletcher-Blake. Angela passed quickly on to other subjects, like saying how sorry she was that Lal had caught pneumonia playing bridge in her bloody draughty house, but I kept going on the subject of Simon Hurst. I said to Angela, "I could have told you when that pampered boy flunked Oxford that he'd never amount to anything, and now, bang, he's headed for a loony bin!"'

There was silence in the kitchen. I'd finished my steak, so I put my knife and fork very carefully together and stared down at my plate. I could feel Hugo looking at me. After a moment, he said, 'What about the child? Didn't Simon have a child?'

'Yes. Disgraceful story,' said Daddy. 'Before your time, Hugo, so you probably don't remember it. The foolish boy got the French girl pregnant, so he had to marry her. Catholic family and all that hoo-ha. The child must be a teenager by now. If she takes after her father, she's probably about to flunk something or other.'

Daddy laughed and took another gulp of wine. Hugo said gently, 'Isn't that a bit severe, Colonel?'

'Well, yes, probably. But I can't abide it when young men have a golden childhood, are given every damn thing they ask for, and then make nothing of their lives. Given a car, he was, the minute he passed his test. In fact, he brought Marianne home from some party in the damn thing one night, didn't he, Mops?'

'Yes,' I said.

'Some malarkey going on between you two, was there?'

'Malarkey?'

'I think there was. I think you told us something about that once. Lucky we went to Cornwall and you met Hugo. Eh?'

'Lucky for me,' said Hugo quickly.

'So, anyway,' said Daddy. 'There you have it. We've got our troubles, but it comforts me to know that the Hursts have got theirs and that theirs are pretty bad. Eh? Isn't there some Kraut word for my shameful delight in their misery: *schadenfreude*?'

I got up and began clearing away the plates. Hugo had bought a pineapple in Harrods, which I'd taken out of the hot kitchen into the larder. This was a joined-on kind of low building, always cool, with marble shelving and wooden racks for storing vegetables and fruit. I went in there and breathed in the perfume of last autumn's apples and remembered that I'd always found this scent very beautiful.

After Hugo left, I told Daddy I would clean Hastings House from top to bottom and make everything shining again. He said, 'Good show, Mops.'

As I lugged the hoover around and fell to my knees to dust the skirting boards and polish all the little legs of the furniture, my mind made the kinds of pictures it had fashioned long ago, imagining what Simon was doing from moment to moment, now that he'd returned to Berkshire. Sometimes, I put him in the garden, sitting in a deckchair, with his long legs stretched out and a book in his hands. He was trying – and failing – to read the book. Sometimes, Marigold Hurst came out into the garden with a jug of lemonade and she and Simon had a quiet, affectionate conversation. Sometimes, he went on solitary walks to Squirrels' Tump, with the wind blowing his hair into his eyes, then he sat down at the top of the tump, near the place where the beech woods began, and he looked down over the silent fields, as though the fields were his past life spread out before him. When he got home from his walks, his mother would look at him in a piercing kind of way, wondering if the fresh air had cured him of the anguish he was feeling. But it didn't cure him. He would go to his room, which still had his boyhood model aeroplanes suspended from the ceiling on bits of fuse wire, and look around at everything and perhaps pick up some old forgotten object, like a pencil case or a broken torch, and wonder if these things should be thrown away, but then replace them in the exact spot where he'd found them.

I was so immersed in my imaginings of Simon's life that the huge burden of housework I'd taken on didn't seem like a burden any more. Scouring baths, washing lino, moving beds to vacuum underneath them, reaching up to cobwebs on the ceilings with a feather duster, even trying to return lavatory bowls to something like a bearable state . . . none of this felt arduous, and I began to tell myself that once all the cleaning was done, I would put clean sheets on Mummy's bed and lay out her favourite white nightdress from Bartlett's and her white bedjacket tied with pink ribbons, so that everything would be ready for when she came home, and when I'd done all this, I would go down to the hall telephone and pick it up and dial Simon's number.

I'd almost completed my tasks and had even got out the sheets for Mummy's bed, when Daddy got the call from the hospital. They told him Mummy had gone into

Intensive Care, but that they were afraid she was 'slipping away'. When Daddy put the phone down, his face had gone a peculiar shade of suet grey. He said, 'I can't lose her, Mops. I simply can't. That was never on the cards. I was the one going to die first. That was never the ruddy deal!'

Daddy was too shocked to drive, so we got into my Renault 4 and bounced along the lanes to Pangbourne, then on to Reading. As I handled the strangely located gearstick, Daddy said, 'This doesn't feel like a normal car,' and I said, 'Well, concentrate on that, then, Daddy, on the surprising oddity of certain material objects.' And Daddy said, 'Well, what I could concentrate on are the ruddy peculiar things you've always said. I've often wondered if you're really my child or if your father isn't some eccentric old fool living halfway up a Greek mountainside or in a tree house on the Isle of Mull.'

I didn't comment on this, but I thought about it for a while and about how the Greek mountainside might look in its rugged glory, as we went along in silence. Then I brought myself back to the here and now, with all the familiar fields and red-brick houses flickering slowly past in the sunlight and keeping us company.

Near the hospital entrance there was a foyer-type place, where there were potted plants and a portrait of the Queen, and the Indian doctor and the ward sister were standing around here, looking apprehensive, as if they were waiting for the actual Queen to arrive. But they weren't waiting for the Queen: they were waiting for us.

They stood very still and straight and the earthly god looked down his fine nose at us and told us that Mummy had died.

I held on to Daddy. His right hand gyrated frantically over his tweed jacket, fumbling for the pocket where his cigarettes might be. He found them and stuffed a du Maurier into his mouth, then began searching for his lighter. A prominent sign above a reception desk said *No Smoking*. I said, 'You can't smoke here, Daddy,' and he said, 'Bugger that,' and found his lighter and lit his cigarette. I thought the god might say that we mortals were honour bound to obey hospital rules, but he didn't. He asked us if we wanted to see Mummy before her body was taken to the mortuary and Daddy said, 'Where the hell is she?' and the ward sister smiled a gentle smile.

'She's in a quiet little side room that we keep for times like these. And let me just tell you that your wife died very peacefully. She didn't suffer.'

'No. All right,' said Daddy. 'But I suppose you imagine that that's enough to comfort me. Do you? Do you? Lal may not have suffered, or so you say, but *I'm* suffering! We were married for thirty-five years. Why the hell did you let her die?'

The god stood very still and didn't recoil from Daddy, who had tugged himself free of my arm and was marching about, looking as though he wanted to stab the enemy with a fixed bayonet. The god said, 'Pulmonary failure prevents oxygen from reaching the brain, Colonel. We did everything we could, but in cases like this one, death will always follow.'

Daddy looked helpless then, like a child who wants to scream but can't remember how. Nobody looked at me or asked if I was all right, and I thought, Well, this is OK because I really don't know if I'm all right or not. I'll just wait to see Mummy and then perhaps I'll know.

We followed the god and the sister down a long corridor. We stopped in front of a door, which had a *Staff Only* sign on it. Then we went in. The frail hospital curtains had been drawn, so the room was shadowy, despite the bright day outside. Mummy lay on her back, with a white blanket pulled up to her neck, so that all we could see of her was her face. Her hair had been brushed straight back, and I found this troubling because it was never how she'd worn it; she liked to have two little curls, like baby horns, caressing her forehead, one on either side, rather like the style the Queen has always favoured. There was a stench of something medicated in the air and I didn't like to think what it was. I wished there could have been some sweet peas – Mummy's favourite flower – scenting the room, but I knew that the season for sweet peas was long over.

Daddy and I stood side by side, looking down at Mummy. The god and the nurse retreated and went out, leaving us alone. Daddy seemed to forget about his cigarette and it began to burn down in his hand, dropping ash onto the lino floor. He said nothing and didn't move. I found I was staring at Mummy's mouth, on which somebody had put a smear of red lipstick. I couldn't help remembering that the last words Mummy had spoken to me were 'Go on.' And I wanted to say, 'Well, yes, I will go on. I've always tried to – in some way or another. But I just don't know, from here, what direction my life is going to take.'

About the loss of my mother, I couldn't seem to summon any grief for myself, just grief for Daddy, who was trying to conduct himself like the old soldier that he was, but with tears running down his war-torn cheeks. I tried to take his hand, but he pushed me away and said, 'We can't stay, Mops. We can't stay and witness this any longer.' Then he put his lips on Mummy's forehead and whispered to her an old joke they'd shared ever since a long-ago holiday in Italy, when they'd asked a friend in Rome how you said 'See you later, alligator/In a while, crocodile' in Italian.

'*Arrivederci, alligatore*,' he said, and stood there, waiting for Mummy to speak. 'Say it, Lal,' he implored. 'Say it, darling: *in un momento, coccodrillo*.'

Then there was the funeral.

As Daddy and Hugo and I stood in the church porch in Weston Applegate to shake the hands of the mourners, I saw, as if from a long way off, Marigold and Christopher Hurst coming down the path and with them were Jasmine and Simon.

Nearer and nearer Simon came. He looked much older, but his hair was still thick and he walked with the same easy grace that used to fascinate my teenage soul. When he saw me, he mouthed my name silently.

Jasmine ran to me and hugged me and said, 'I know we weren't invited, but we wanted to come. For your sake.'

Then Simon came forward. He stood in front of me, not knowing what to do, his regard flickering anxiously towards Hugo. Jasmine said, 'For goodness' sake, Simon, give Marianne a hug.' But he didn't move. He just looked at me with a puzzled expression on his face, like somebody trying to work out a complicated equation. I put out a hand, encased in a black glove, and touched his shoulder, but he took my hand from it, seeming not to want it there, and said, 'Perhaps you didn't recognise me?'

'Of course I recognised you,' I said. I wanted to say, 'I recognised you because I've never left you. I followed you as you walked around Paris. I saw you climbing your stairs and standing at a window and closing the shutters. I went into the café where you liked to drink a little espresso and after you'd drunk it, I held the china cup in my hands. I strolled along beside you when you took your daughter for a walk by the Seine and bought a *beignet* for her from a street vendor. I was in your bed when you made love to your wife . . .'

Instead of coming out with all this, I said, 'I don't think you've met my husband, Hugo,' and I watched, in a kind of terrified stupor, as Simon and Hugo shook hands and smiled politely at each other. Then I said, 'You remember Daddy, Simon?' And I seemed to know exactly what we were both remembering: how Daddy had quizzed Simon about his car on the night of Rowena's hop, on the night I lost my virginity in a Morris parked in a sighing wood.

Daddy stared at Simon. Simon held out the hand Hugo had relinquished, but Daddy didn't take it. Since Mummy's death, I didn't know, from one moment to the next, whether Daddy was going to do or say something normal or something completely crazy and rude, and now he said, 'Simon, is it? The one who flunked Oxford?'

Simon gaped. Jasmine stepped in and said, 'That was long ago, Colonel Clifford,' and Daddy said, '*Everything* is long ago, young lady. When you get to my age you will understand this. Every darn thing is past and gone.'

Jasmine looked baffled. She took Simon's hand and said, 'I think we'd better go into the church and find a seat.' And she led him away. Marigold and Christopher were left to confront Daddy, and Marigold said, in her soft and soothing voice, 'Atrocious luck, Colonel. We're very, very sorry,' and before Daddy could say anything more, the Hursts hurried away from him.

When all the funeral guests had filed in, Hugo and Daddy and I walked up the aisle of the church where Anthracite and I had got married and went into our pew. Pet waited here to be a kind of maid of honour at Mummy's funeral, just as she'd been a maid of honour at my wedding, but this time she had a tartan beret on her wild hair instead of the floral bagel she'd had to wear all those years ago. I held on to her arm. I whispered, 'Simon's turned up. I'm having difficulty breathing.'

Pet tugged me towards her and held me close. I could feel that she wanted to say something, but didn't know what, or else didn't dare say anything which Hugo might overhear. Then the choir filed in, sweet little cherubs of boys with round faces above white ruffs, and we all stood up to sing 'Morning Has Broken', which was Mummy's favourite hymn. As we sang, my thoughts slid back and forth between Mummy's body lying in the coffin, with those accustomed little curls of hair absent from her forehead, and the presence of Simon, standing tall and silent, somewhere in the church behind me. I longed to turn round, to see where he was, to send him some kind of yearning message, but I stopped myself from doing this.

I told myself to concentrate on the loss of Mummy and all the things I would never hear her say again. I suppose I was trying to make myself weep, but the tears wouldn't come. I kept remembering how, whenever I told her the things which were in my heart or my head, she'd often preferred not to believe them. When I once said that I could remember lying in my pram as a baby and seeing birds perching on telegraph wires, she'd said, 'Don't be silly, Marianne. Babies remember nothing.' She'd gone through my entire life somehow believing that I was a liar.

There was no eulogy for Mummy. Daddy would have given it, but he said he could no longer get his thoughts into a straight line. And probably I should have done it, but I somehow felt that, whatever I said, my mother would lie in her silk-lined box and whisper, 'This is bunkum. This is rot.' So after a few hymns and prayers for the living and the dead and a repetition of Psalm 23, we all filed out into a field behind the churchyard which was known as the 'overspill cemetery', and we stood around while Mummy was put into the earth. Daddy was wearing his army uniform, too tight for his ageing frame. At the graveside, he took off one of his medals and threw it onto the coffin and said again, '*Arrivederci, alligatore.*'

When all this was done, holding on to Pet and Hugo, I looked around for Simon, but he was gone.

I stayed on at Hastings House after Hugo went back to London and his work at Riley Mountfitchet, not only because Daddy needed someone to clean and cook for him and play Scrabble with him, and let him cry into his whisky, but because I knew that Simon was now living less than five miles away from me and that very soon, something would have to happen between us.

Before Pet left, she said to me, 'You know that's all you've talked about since the funeral: the thing that might or might not happen between you and the paragon. You don't talk about your dead mother.'

'What people tend to talk about the most,' I replied, 'are the things which have the possibility of breaking their hearts. Lavender Clifford broke my heart so long ago by not loving me that I lost all interest in her.'

Pet was sitting in my room, on a tilty little stool that Mummy had bought to go with the dressing table she put in for me when I was fourteen and began to dream about a lipstick called Roman Pink. Pet was far too big for the stool. She rested her elbows on her knees and looked around the room and said, 'This looks to me like a teen-ager's room fitted out with care. If your mother never loved you, why would she have done that?'

'I don't know,' I said. 'She had impeccable taste, I guess. She liked things to look neat and pretty.'

'That's not good enough, Marianne. Perhaps she tried to love you and you never gave her the chance?'

'Wrong.'

'Not necessarily wrong, because after you got married and went away, she kept the room just as it had been when you were in it. Nothing has been moved or taken away. I think that should tell you something.'

'No. It just tells me that she was too lazy or too mean or too worried about money to redecorate it. So what are you saying, Pet?'

I was sitting on the bed, which was still covered with an old white candlewick bedspread. Pet got up from the stool and came and sat beside me and took my hand.

'I think,' she said, 'I'm just saying "be careful". You need to be sure, if you're planning to meet up with Simon again, that you're not going to hurt the people who love you.'

'You're right,' I said, 'except that the people you're thinking of . . . I don't love them back. Not with my whole heart. Neither Hugo, nor Mummy and Daddy, nor anyone. The only people I've ever truly loved are you and Simon and my horse Mirabelle.'

Pet smiled and kissed my hair. I hugged her for that smile and that kiss. I felt so sad that she was soon going to go away. I was sad for two reasons: because I would miss her and because her life was full of purpose and endeavour and when she left, these things would vanish with her and all I would be left with was the autumn winds blowing the birch leaves onto the grass.

And it was difficult being with Daddy. He walked around like a person in a hailstorm, bent over, with his trousers sagging down from his bony rump and sometimes with his hand covering his head. Pity for him began to grow inside me; a little potato sprout of pity I'd never felt for him before.

He didn't talk about Mummy. He didn't seem to want her name brought into the conversation. But he took the faded old photograph of their wedding from a side table in the sitting room and put it by his bed, and I thought, It's not the recent Lal he wants beside him, the one I called Mummy – with the sound of her court shoes echoing on the parquet and her voice becoming shrill – but the young Lal, who was soft to his touch, who had applied a hesitant touch of some dark lipstick to the bridal mouth, who clutched her bouquet of white arum lilies to her heart, as if to shield her from all that she didn't yet know, and who gazed into his eyes with adoration: the Lal he had all to himself before I came along.

One of our tasks was to drive into Hungerford to see the family solicitor, to go over Mummy's will. The solicitor was called Mr Barker, and he was older and even more bent than Daddy, so that when we left him, Daddy said, 'Poor old Barker. Can't bloody well stand up straight any more,' and I had to suppress the peal of laughter I felt inside me.

Not that I had anything to laugh about. Mummy had left her share of Hastings House and her dwindling portfolio of stocks and shares and almost every single thing she owned to Daddy. When Daddy died, it was all to go to some charity for Distressed Gentlefolk. I said to Daddy, 'Who are Distressed Gentlefolk exactly?' And he said,

'People like me, Mops. People who always thought they'd have enough to see them through and then inflation blew in and a farcical government puts up tax and the country starts to hit the buffers.'

I said, 'Well, I hit the buffers in Mummy's will. Didn't I? All I got was five hundred pounds and a Swansea blue tea service.'

'That tea service is valuable,' he said. 'Ask Hugo.'

I talked to Hugo that night. I didn't mention the tea service. I just told him I was a tiny bit-part player in the drama of Mummy's will – almost not there at all. I said, 'What I feel is that the parents would have liked it to be the other way round: for me to have died before them, and then they would have been happy again, like they were at the beginning.'

There was a silence when I said this and I could hear Hugo wondering if what I'd just said was true, or not. After a moment, he said, 'Don't stay any longer, Yeti. Come back to London. Let your father figure out how to cope.' And I almost came out with what was in my head. I almost said, 'I'm not staying on just because Daddy's so bent over and forgetful and wears sagging trousers. I'm staying until the moment arrives . . . the moment so long postponed . . . when I get into my car and drive over to the Hursts . . .' But I heard Pet caution, 'Men don't love like you've loved. They love in relays. One and then another and then another. On the baton goes. And the ones they held long ago, they just lie on the track for some other runner to trip over.'

*

168

I chose a bright, cold day. I left Daddy playing patience in a cheating kind of way, uncovering cards he had no right to reveal. He didn't ask me where I was going. He seemed to have lost all interest in the *reason* for things, just as he'd lost all interest in keeping to the rules of solitary card games.

I drove very slowly, attentive to the bright light and the beauty of the long shadows of the poplar trees. When I pulled up in front of the Hursts' house, I half expected to see Simon's car of long ago sitting in the drive, waiting for me to stroke its baby blue nose.

Marigold answered the door. Her hair was grey and straight, where it had once been brown and curly. A ratty little nondescript dog barked at her feet and Marigold said, 'Sorry about the noise, Marianne. Be quiet, Freddie! Come in and he'll calm down.'

We walked through to the sitting room, which had been redecorated in soothing pastel colours. There was no sign of Christopher or of Simon. On the piano stood multiple photographs of Simon and Jasmine, smiling at the camera as the years passed. Marigold saw me looking at them and said, 'I expect you came to see Simon?'

'Well, yes. I wanted to talk to him at Mummy's funeral, but you left after the service.'

Marigold stood very still, holding on to the shiny piano lid, looking at me in a sorrowful kind of way. Then she said very quietly, 'I'm upset about your mother. We would have come to the reception after the funeral, but Simon felt we weren't going to be welcome.'

'I would have welcomed you.'

'I know you would. But Simon was shocked by what your father said to him.'

'Yes,' I said. 'I'm really sorry. I was shocked, too. But Daddy sometimes says inappropriate things. He always has.'

'I understand. Perhaps we all say things we don't mean from time to time? And now you've come to see Simon?'

'Yes.'

Marigold let go of the piano lid and stood with her arms folded, like a person preparing to square up to something unforeseen.

'Simon's not here,' she said. 'I'm very sorry that you've come all this way. He's gone back to London.'

'Ah.'

'He left a few days ago, but he said . . .'

'He said?'

'He said, if you called . . . well, he said he thought you might call . . .'

'Yes?'

'He told me how fond of you he's always been and how much, over the years, he's thought about you. He wanted me to explain some important things to you.'

'What things, Marigold?'

'I'll tell you, Marianne, but look, I was just about to take Freddie for a walk. Why don't I get my coat and we can go up to Squirrels' Tump. The day looks rather fine, doesn't it. Will your shoes manage the tump?'

I looked down at my shoes. I'd put on some narrow, flat pumps I'd had for years. I'd had them so long, I thought Simon might remember them and be moved by the sight of my feet. Now I thought how stupid that was – that thought along with a thousand others which had occupied my brain for so long. I told Marigold I had some wellingtons in the car and I'd wear these. I waited while she tied a silk headscarf round her grey hair and clipped a lead onto Freddie, who was now yelping with gladness.

I pulled the wellingtons out of the car boot. We set off over a field towards the tump. The sound and feel of the wellingtons flubbing against my legs reminded me of being a girl. I said, 'Do you remember the day of Jasmine's scavenger hunt, when you said we might find Saxon arrowheads?'

'Did I say that?' said Marigold. 'I suppose it's one of the wonderful things about having children: they let you tease them.' Then she said that she supposed I would have children by now and when I told her that my baby had died after I fell from a horse on a beach in Cornwall, she said, 'Oh goodness, Marianne, what a tragedy for you. We had no idea. I'm so sorry. Sometimes I wish we could all go back to things as they were: we could call it Saxon Arrowhead Time, a little Berkshire Eden.'

'What?' I said. 'Then start over again, differently?'

'Yes, I think that's what I mean. I suppose it probably is.'

When we got to the top of the tump, Marigold led me to a fallen tree at the very edge of the wood. She said, 'I like to sit here and have a little rest after the hill. I used not to need the rest, but now I do.'

Freddie seemed to know about the pause in the walk.

He came and sat obediently at Marigold's feet and we gazed down over the valley, at the dark oaks and the hedgerows burdened with haw berries, and Marigold said, 'Now I'm going to tell you about Simon.'

I waited. The wind was quite strong and blew my hair into my eyes. Marigold said, 'Simon thought that his father and I would be shocked by what's happened, but I told him that we'd understood years ago. He fell in love when he was at school, aged eighteen. The boy was Indian. Very, very clever and with the kind of beauty it's difficult to quantify. He told me that the moment he saw this boy, he knew that he'd love him absolutely and forever. That's what he said: "absolutely and forever".

'And so it's turned out, you see. Being Simon, as kind a person as he is and always wanting to please everybody, he tried to put his feelings for the boy aside. He tried to love girls. I think he tried really hard. I know he was very fond of you, in particular, Marianne. He said he had such fun with you. And then he was trapped by what happened with Solange. He saw out many years with her. I don't doubt that he tried to be a good husband and father. But those kinds of things are absolutes. We all know that. He couldn't forget what he felt for the Indian boy. And now . . .'

'I know his name,' I said. 'It's Amar Nath Chatterjee.'

'Yes. Rather hard to pronounce it properly, I find, but I expect that's my ignorance. Simon calls him "Achille", but that's just his pet name for him. It's been very difficult for Solange and the little girl, who are hurt and confused and want to punish Simon. I understand that they can't

172

accept it; Simon belonged to them for so many years, or so they thought. But Christopher and I have accepted it. What else could we do? Simon's wrestled with this for far, far too long, but we saw that it was beginning to unhinge him. He was trying to write a book, but the book wasn't working. He was too unhappy and agitated to make anything work. I felt such sorrow for him. I said to him, "For God's sake, darling, go and be with your beloved Achille and recover your sanity and be happy." I think I was right, don't you?'

I wanted to say to Marigold that I was sure she was right, but I found that I couldn't speak. I listened to the wind sighing in the wood behind us and began thinking of how, quite soon, the snow would make ghosts of all the beech trees. Marigold reached out and put her arm around me. Freddie looked up and gave a little whine, perhaps not liking that Marigold's arm was holding me and not him, and I thought how perplexing it was that every sentient creature is in thrall to some kind of yearning.

Then I stared numbly down at the familiar valley, at the oaks and the haw berries, and I tried to imagine what Amar Nath Chatterjee would look like, in all his beauty and strangeness. But I knew that whatever picture of him my mind conjured, it probably wouldn't be real and true. What would be real and true would be the tenderness of Simon's regard, a regard which had fallen on me so long ago. I could clearly picture the way he would caress his lover with his eyes, the way this glance would follow him as he moved, the way lovemaking would sometimes overwhelm him and make him weep.

I bent down and stroked the dog and his bright button eyes looked up at me pleadingly. I found my voice at last and said to Marigold, 'That "forever" thing. Lots of people don't believe it, but I know that it's true.'

I stayed on with Daddy at Hastings House through Christmas and into the spring. I spent a lot of time on my knees, cleaning out the grime of years. I felt I wanted to cry all day and every day and all night and every night, but I never did. I just carried on, moment to moment.

I'd begun to be afraid of going back to London. I pretended to Hugo that I kept trying to leave Daddy but that he threw all the Scrabble tiles onto the floor when I mentioned it and wouldn't let me go. On the telephone, Pet said to me, 'Enough house cleaning. Now's the time when you have to clean up your future.'

I said to Pet, 'What do you mean, exactly?'

'It means . . . I'll tell you what I think it means, because I've given a lot of thought to this: you need to set Hugo free.'

I lay in my old room, trying not to dream. The linen sheets I slept in were thin and worn. I thought, Pet is right. Hugo should be free to be with someone else, someone who can give him children and love him properly.

I went to Daddy and I said, 'If I left Hugo, could I stay on here – at least until . . .'

'Until what?'

'I don't know. Until I can see my way forward.'

Daddy and I were sitting by the fire, getting drunk. He was drinking brandy and soda and I was drinking vodka and tonic and we were at that stage of drunkenness when things creep into the human mind that it doesn't often feel – hope and remorse and sudden love.

Daddy refreshed our glasses, sloshing in much more vodka than tonic, much more brandy than water, and said, 'I know I've been unfair to you, Mops. Never given you credit for much, never thought you'd amount to anything I could be proud of. But since Mummy went, I've seen that you're kind. And that's not nothing. That is far from nothing, because not many people are . . .'

'Well,' I said, 'I can be unkind, too.'

'Don't interrupt,' said Daddy. 'I've been thinking that you've had a rum deal with the house. The whole place is collapsing into the proverbial log basket, but never mind. You can still hear doves in the birch tree. Or are they pigeons? I don't know. I was always nil at Nature Studies. But look, let's go and see old Bent-Over Barker and get things straightened out a bit. I'll give you Granny Violet's emerald choker now and you can sell it or keep it, just as the fancy takes you. And when I pop off you can have some more stuff, and you can have the house.'

'Thank you, Daddy,' I said. 'That's very fair of you. But what about the Distressed Gentlefolk?'

'Bugger them,' said Daddy. 'Why pander to strangers? I prefer you to have the house. Hugo will help you to renovate it.'

I took another gulp of my vodka. 'The thing is,' I said, 'I'm probably going to leave Hugo. This is what I've been trying to tell you.'

'Leave Hugo?' said Daddy. 'Why would you do that?'

'Because I think he deserves a chance at life without me.'

Daddy took a huge swig of his brandy and fixed me with his colonel's eye, glittery and fierce as a bullet.

'Get on old Hugo's nerves, do you?' he said. 'Or what? What the hell is all this leaving business?'

'I expect I do get on his nerves,' I said, 'but it's more complicated than that. It's more that I think he should be able to start again with someone else.'

'Someone else? He married *you*, I seem to remember. Didn't I pay for a vast quantity of beef Wellington?'

'You did. And we made quite a good fist of the marriage. But it's come to me lately that Hugo deserves a chance to be with someone who can give him children.'

Now, Daddy's glittery eye blinked and his head jerked upwards, as though with sudden fright at the sound of a distant rifle shot.

'Oh,' he said. 'Forgot about all that! Clean forgot. The children thing. Oh Lord. Stupid me. Rum show, my poor Mops. Rum show.'

'Yes, it was a rum show.'

Daddy took his drink and began to pace about the room. With his face turned away from me, he said, 'Never told you this, Marianne, but your mother and I . . . when that terrible thing happened to you, I knew exactly what you and Hugo were feeling because Lal and I . . . we went through that same dreadful type of saga before you were born.'

'What, Daddy? What are you saying?'

'Same saga as yours. Except we lost a baby boy. At six

176

or seven months, I can't remember. About three years before we had you. Lal was inconsolable. I think, if you asked me to be honest about it, she never quite got over it. We were going to call the little boy Simon.'

Now, it went completely quiet in the room. I clutched my vodka glass. The voice I heard in my mind was Pet's and she was angry. She said, 'Oh for heaven's sake, why wasn't this told to you years ago, Marianne? Doesn't it explain so fucking much? Why did that fucking generation keep everything hidden away behind the fucking arras?'

I looked over towards Daddy, who was still turned away from me. For a moment, I wished Pet could have been there in the room to give Daddy's head a vicious clout with her sturdy Scottish fist. But then I told myself that really, it was too late for anger, everybody was just too tired, too scarred and bleeding. So I just said, in a calm voice: 'I wish you could have told me about that, Daddy. Told me when I was much younger . . .'

Daddy took a gulp of his drink and said, 'I don't know what that would have served. We all got through, didn't we, the three of us? We struggled on through.'

'I suppose we did . . .'

'No, we did, we did. You, me and Mummy. But now Lal's gone and just when everything's disintegrating, you're telling me that you're going to leave poor old Hugo. What is this? Dunkirk?'

'Yes,' I said quietly. 'But you don't need reminding, Daddy, that men were saved at Dunkirk. That was the whole point of it, to save people to fight another day.'

'All right, all right, but what "other day" have you got? What's going to happen to you?'

'I'm going to look after you. You can't eat frozen pheasant forever.'

'Kind of you, Mops, truly kind, but that's no life for you, looking after an old curmudgeon like me.'

'It's a perfectly good life. We'll eat lots of those fried potatoes that you love. I'll start a vegetable patch in the garden. But also, I've got a little project to take my mind off all the sad and difficult things that have happened. I've begun a bit of work: a story for kids about a horse . . . Perhaps something will come of that.'

Daddy shook his head. He ran an anxious hand through his white hair, which had got very long and unkempt, and said, 'Doesn't sound likely to me. Nobody should put their hope in stories, Mops. If I was you, I'd give all that up and stay with old Hugo. I really would. I'll manage fine on my own and Hugo's a better bet than a horse. Isn't he?'

But Pet was right. When I told Hugo I was leaving, he didn't look particularly surprised. He said, 'I watched you lingering on and on with your father, so it wasn't difficult to figure out that you might never come back. I suppose there's somebody else, is there?'

'No,' I said. 'It's not that. It's that Pet told me I should set you free – to marry a new person and have children before it's too late – and I think she's right. I'm doing it out of affection for you, Anthracite.'

He looked sad, but not in a haunted kind of way. I

178

wondered if there was already somebody else in his life, but I didn't ask him if there was. He said he thought that we'd behaved honourably towards each other. We'd tried 'like grown-ups' to have a decent marriage, but the loss of the baby had been very hard and things had never been the same as they'd been in Cornwall, when we'd dressed up in furs to play ping-pong.

He asked me if I was going to be lonely without him and I said, 'Well, yes, I'm sure there will be times when I am, in fact probably lots of times, because I really like you, Anthracite. Also, Daddy is becoming as mad as a March hare, but I'm going to try not to be too distracted by that and to concentrate on my work.'

'What work?' he said. 'Your thing about the Argentinian horse?'

'Yes.'

'Do you call that "work" exactly, Yeti?'

'What else should I call it?'

'I don't know. Work usually *leads* somewhere, to an actual goal, but I can't really see this leading anywhere, can you? Isn't it just fantasy?'

I shrugged. I said that I didn't know but that I wasn't keen to go on with this conversation. I put my arms around Hugo and hugged him and he hugged me back. He said he would send me some money, but I told him I didn't want any money. I had Mummy's five hundred pounds and Granny Violet's emerald choker to sell and I was going to try to get back my old job at Bartlett's, doing gift wrap. I said, 'That's the level of my usefulness at the moment: wrapping other people's presents, just like I'm wrapping you with my arms, ready for someone else.'

Then I went out of the flat and down the stairs and got into the car with the Adler sitting faithfully beside me. As I drove towards Berkshire, I wasn't thinking about leaving my life with Hugo, I was making decisions about how my story would go on.

I decided that Diego would manage to get out of the shed where the boy has abandoned him. He escapes by rearing up and tugging free the wooden bar to which his halter is tethered. For a long time, he runs wild on the pampas, grazing on clover, drinking from foaming little streams, but the wooden bar is still attached to the rope halter and the bar keeps striking his flesh as he moves and begins to wound him.

Diego goes on and on searching for the boy who left him, but he doesn't find him. He's captured by a posse of rancheros who put him to work, rounding up cattle. The rancheros cut the halter and take the wooden bar away and treat Diego's wounds with poultices made from some special plant found only in the Amazonian rainforest. They have the feeling that the horse should be grateful for their care. And yet Diego isn't grateful, because that's the way of the world. Tired from running the cattle, he lies down in the dust and tells us: *The piece of wood was the last bit of proof that I'd ever belonged to the boy and it had hurt me and made a wound in my side, but now I miss it. It seems very stupid to miss a piece of wood and yet I do.*

Trying to keep all this together in my mind was very tiring. It distracted me from the drive so much that I missed my exit from the M4. Realising this, I felt almost surprised that my faithful little car hadn't known the way on its own by now, but it hadn't, and so together we had to take Junction 13 and cut back towards Weston Applegate via Chieveley.

penguin.co.uk/vintage